Miranda's Choice

By Mya O'Malley

*For my mom, Trisia and my daughter,
Alexandra, who both know how much I love
mermaids.
Thank you for all of your love and support.*

Prologue

Whoosh!

Miranda sucked in saltwater as a wave crashed over her head. Gasping for air, the small child tried to scream for help but ended up swallowing even more water in the process. Sand, seaweed, and debris swirled as the child felt a pull, helplessly dragged under the water by the strong current.

Feeling something dragging her to the surface, Miranda gave in to the sensation of floating upward, seeking sunlight and fresh air. After choking on the saltwater that had nearly filled her lungs, Miranda was focused on one thing only: the need to breathe.

The wait seemed endless, but finally she surfaced. She could breathe!

Rubbing salt from her eyes, Miranda was rewarded with the vision of captivating blue-green eyes that seemed to suck her in. They were all she could see.

"Shh! It's okay, sweetie. My name is Abigail. Don't be afraid." The woman reached out her hand to touch the little girl's face. Miranda goggled the way only a three-year-old child could. The sound of the woman's voice was pure delight: awe and curiosity rolled into one.

"Abby," she attempted.

The woman let out a sweet, melodic laugh. "Sure, honey, you can call me Abby. What's your name?"

Miranda looked around, searching for her parents, but knew instinctively that this woman had saved her life. "Miranda," she answered meekly.

"Well, Miranda, you're safe now. Go back to your mom and dad—but please, be more careful from now on, you hear?" Abigail instructed, gazing at the child.

The mysterious woman turned to swim away, but Miranda grabbed at her hand.

"No, don't go! Will I see you again?" The woman's beauty took the little girl's breath away.

Abigail hesitated a brief moment before turning to face the child. "I'll tell you what. If you find you ever need me, simply say this rhyme: 'If I need you, I'll let it be, if you need me, look to the sea.'"

Miranda scrunched her brows in confusion as she tried to make sense of the simple rhyme. She tried to repeat it but forgot the verses immediately. "Abby!"

But Abby had turned to swim off. She splashed as she moved toward the horizon, disappearing into the dark blue water. The last thing that Miranda saw was what appeared to be a large greenish fin.

Before she could understand what she had just seen, her thoughts were disrupted by the sound of her mother's voice.

"Miranda! Thanks goodness!" Miranda's mother ran into the water, closing the distance between them. She scooped her daughter into her arms and squeezed her for all she was worth. Miranda tried to speak, opening her mouth to tell her mother about the pretty blonde woman with the sparkling eyes, but somehow the words wouldn't come.

Chapter One

"Come on. Truth or dare," Eve insisted. "What's it going to be?" She sat tapping her fingers on the table, her eyes raised to the ceiling.

Eve was always trying to get her to play this game lately, and Miranda just wasn't into it. At thirteen, she did not wish to divulge any secrets, nor did she want to be made a fool of, as she was sure Eve would do if she were to accept a dare.

"How about we play a different game? Or watch TV? Our show is on," Miranda suggested, knowing that Eve could never resist finding out what happened to Michael and Melanie on their favorite sitcom.

"Yeah! Let's find out what Melanie decides!" Eve grinned, jumping up from her seat at the table.

Whew. She had averted the game once more. Miranda enjoyed Eve's company, but sometimes her best friend really got on her nerves. Eve Rand had to have everything her way or the highway. Miranda considered herself far from perfect, but at least she could roll with the punches when required.

"Miranda!" Her mother's voice could be heard coming from upstairs.

Oh, no. She had forgotten to clean her room again. Miranda cringed, knowing what was coming.

"Get ready for it: three, two, one..." Miranda whispered, counting the descending numbers on her hand.

Eve was oblivious, her eyes glued to the television screen now playing their show, her bottom planted to the carpeted floor of the living room.

"Miranda Mae!" the voice sounded. "I thought you told me that your room was cleaned!" Her mother's footsteps could be heard on the stairs, and then she appeared in the doorway, hands on her hips, a frown creasing her otherwise pretty face.

"Mom, I'm sorry, I just kind of forgot." Miranda attempted to charm her mom with a half smile and a shrug.

"I told you that Eve could not come over if your room wasn't cleaned."

At the sound of her name, Eve turned and waved to Miranda's mom. "Hey, Mrs. James."

Miranda always wondered why her friend addressed her mom with the title "Mrs." when she knew Miranda's parents had divorced years earlier. She supposed that "Miss James," or calling her by her first name, Anne, would sound even odder.

"Hi, Eve," her mother responded. "I'm very sorry, but Miranda needs to clean up her room, so you'll have to go back home. You may come back today when she has finished—or I should say, *if* she finishes." A firm line was set on her face and her eyebrows were knitted. Miranda knew that her mom meant business.

Talk about embarrassing me in front of my friend! With a huff, Miranda threw up her hands and looked at Eve.

"See you later. I'll call you," she mumbled, heading upstairs.

"Miranda, you have nobody to blame but yourself, you know," her mother called after her as Eve closed the front door behind her.

Slamming her own door to the bedroom, Miranda kicked some of her clothes across the room. It wasn't such a big deal that Eve had been sent home—her friend only lived several houses away and seemed to be a permanent fixture around Miranda's house lately. But why couldn't her mom be cool like her friend Stephanie's mom? Stephanie's mom had great fashion sense, she let them eat ice cream at midnight when Miranda slept over, and Stephanie's room was always a disaster, worse than her own. Miranda lay on her clothes-ridden bedspread and stared up at the ceiling.

"Are you finished yet?" Her mom was outside the door. Glancing at the time on her phone, Miranda realized that a half an hour had flown by with her doing nothing. Her room was still a mess.

"Hello?" Her mother nudged the door open, glancing inside. "Hm. It looks as if Eve won't be coming back today."

Miranda continued to gaze upward, pretending to ignore her mother's words.

"Fine, be that way. Dinner will be ready in about two hours." Her mother closed the door softly.

Not for the first time, Miranda imagined what life would be like if she lived with her dad across town. Her dad was very cool, but you couldn't forget the "Sarah factor," as Miranda called it. Sarah was Dad's new girlfriend. The woman was a good ten years younger than her father, which would make her about thirty.

Recalling the first time that she had met the woman, Miranda scrunched up her face in disgust. Her father had taken them to dinner at her favorite restaurant, Michelle's. Sarah had downright ruined her baked tortellini dinner with her long, black hair and overly made-up eyes. Sure, Sarah had tried to be nice, but Miranda saw right through the farce.

Weren't they all so nice and sweet until they got to know you?

The last thing Miranda needed was a stepmother. Sarah and her dad hadn't been dating for *that* long, but she'd heard of these things happening fast. *One minute you're going to your dad's house on the weekends, everything is great, your dad dotes all over you—and then, bam! Some teenage wannabe takes your place, moving in on your dad with her smiles and sweetness.* If Miranda had anything to do with it, she would make sure that the woman never got any ideas about moving in or marrying her dad.

* * *

"Aren't you coming with us?" her dad called up to her room at his house.

Miranda loved her room here. It was slightly larger than her room at Mom's house, and here she had her own gaming system on the larger flatscreen television. Her mother warned her that buying more expensive things didn't mean anything when it came to raising a child.

Deep down, Miranda knew this to be true. Miranda's mom had always tried her best to provide a good home and stability for her daughter and son. It wasn't fair that she had to go back to work after staying home for so many years to raise her and David alone.

Miranda had been young when her parents separated, but she still remembered overhearing the argument one night when her parents thought she was asleep. Mom had accused Dad of having a girlfriend. Dad had denied it at first, screaming that she was crazy and everything, but Mom insisted.

She kept saying that she knew, and finally Dad gave in and admitted it. He actually *admitted* it, but said he didn't want to leave.

Miranda had been particularly close with her dad. She was his little girl. She had sobbed into her pillow that night, unable to believe that her dad could hurt her, her mother, and David, too. She knew her parents had basically just ignored each other—but she had assumed this was the way it was. Parents were too old to be in love, right?

But then again, Eve's parents kissed all the time and actually hung out together. Stephanie's parents were divorced, but Hilary's mom and dad were always going out on date nights. Miranda figured then that her mom and dad were in real trouble. The divorce just cemented the fact in her mind.

It was living without him that was the tough part. The killer was, the woman had never even meant anything to her dad—she had helped destroy his family, but he broke up with her shortly afterwards. (Eavesdropping on her mother's phone calls to her girlfriends was Miranda's primary source for information, even now.)

"No, Dad. I'm good." *There's no way I'm going out with him and Sarah.*

"Miranda, open the door." *Do they not realize how annoying it is that they constantly ask to speak with me, to open the door?*

"What?" She flung the door open, standing with her hand planted on her hip.

"Don't speak to me like that, young lady." His tone was firm.

"Sorry," she mumbled. She really didn't like upsetting her father, but her feelings for him were all tangled up inside. Miranda's mom had insisted that she go to a therapist for a while after the divorce. At first she had resisted, and then she had blamed both her parents for the divorce. For a brief period, she had even blamed herself. Years later, she knew she needed to forgive and forget, and to love both of her parents, even though they were obviously flawed.

"It would mean a lot to me, to Sarah, if you came with us." He smiled down at her, rubbing her head just like he used to.

"Fine," she muttered, turning back into her room to get ready.

"That's my girl." Dad walked back to his room, calling for Sarah to start up the car.

Chapter Two

It was freezing. What was her father thinking? They should have just stayed home and ordered take-out or something. The heater wasn't quite reaching the back seat yet, but Miranda was pretty sure that Sarah was plenty warm up front beside her father.

"How's school?" Sarah spun her long black hair to face Miranda.

"Fine." Miranda barely opened her mouth to respond but then caught her dad's face in the rearview mirror.

"What's that?" Sarah leaned back, holding her hand to her ear.

"It's fine, it's good." She spoke louder, enunciating every word. Her father's eyes were back on the road and he reached over for Sarah's hand. *Really? Right in front of me?* Miranda rolled her eyes and wondered why they couldn't control themselves for at least one evening.

Pulling her phone from her pocket, Miranda studied a message from Eve. "Out with dad and his precious little witch of a girlfriend," she texted, then sighed and shoved the phone back into her pocket. It looked as if they had arrived at the Mexican restaurant.

The cold winter air slapped Miranda's cheeks as she pressed her jacket closer to her chest. Her dad stepped out of the car, patted her back and then caught up with Sarah, grabbing her hand. A moment of sadness hit Miranda, as suddenly as the cold air had slapped her seconds before. Her father could have put in this kind of effort with her mother years ago. Perhaps if he did, they would still be a family. What she was seeing before her just proved to her how messed up her life was.

Am I jealous? Yes, probably, but she also felt bad for her mom. Miranda's mom hadn't so much as dated, and now her dad had this relationship with a younger woman.

"Honey?" Her father slowed down and reached for her with his free arm. *No way, they were not a happy little family.* Shrugging him off, Miranda stepped ahead, not caring to witness the icy stare she was sure was coming her way.

Hearing her dad clear his throat and whisper something to Sarah, she opened the door and waited by the entrance. Her dad and Sarah were two steps behind.

"Three?" The host came toward them, grabbing menus, and ushered them to a table in the back of the room.

Her father pulled Sarah's chair out for her and kissed her lightly on the forehead. Smiling from ear to ear, Sarah kissed him back and then sat down. Miranda smirked, feeling oddly out of place. Tossing her phone on the table with a thud, she excused herself to go to the bathroom.

Had her father gone crazy? Didn't he see that this woman was going to cause problems with their relationship? Splashing some water on her face, Miranda gazed at her reflection in the mirror. Her blonde hair fell across her forehead, covering her dark blue eyes. Scrunching her face, she sized herself up, criticizing her fair skin smattered with freckles. Pulling at her cheeks, she realized for the hundredth time that, try as she might, her freckles were there to stay.

Walking back to the table, Miranda spied her father rubbing Sarah's back, her face pointing down toward the table. *What was her problem?*

Pulling out her own chair, Miranda settled herself at the table.

"How could you be so insensitive?" her father demanded. "Sarah has been nothing but kind to you."

What was this about?

He shoved her cell phone at her. Miranda gasped and snatched it. What had they seen?

"Go ahead, check your messages." Her father's voice resonated hurt.

Miranda hit the message button in the corner of the screen. It was a response from Eve: "Have fun with the wicked witch. Don't worry, she'll probably be gone before you know it."

Daring a look at her father, the wheels were turning. Could she pretend that she had been talking about someone else? But who?

Apparently she wasn't quick enough. Her father spoke again.

"You owe Sarah an apology. I'll deal with you when we get home." He eyed her harshly.

Seconds away from muttering an apology to Sarah, it hit her.

"Wait a minute. Why were you guys even looking at my phone?" she demanded, looking back and forth between the two. Sarah had tears in her eyes and her father just looked furious.

"Excuse me, young lady? Who do you think you're talking to? I should have known that your mother allows this behavior. Well, guess what? *My* house, *my* rules! You want to come over, you respect Sarah!" he boomed.

She couldn't believe her ears. Customers at a nearby table stared at them, silent. Standing up, she grabbed her phone.

"I. Am. Out. Of. Here," she snapped.

"Sit back down." Her father lowered his voice, glancing around the restaurant. Miranda slowly lowered herself to her chair, her heart beating like a drum in her chest.

"I'm waiting," her father said. He tapped his fingers on the table while Sarah turned away.

"That was my *private* message," she stated, looking straight at Sarah, who now met her gaze with her head up.

"You left it on the table. I couldn't help but see it when the message came through," Sarah challenged.

"It was none of your business!" Miranda hissed through clenched teeth.

"Enough!" her father barked. "Enough, young lady. Apologize at once."

He was taking her side, her side. "Sorry." She kept her head down, mumbling the apology. This was going to be the worst dinner ever.

"Apology accepted. Miranda, believe it or not, I'm not the enemy," Sarah said softly. *What? What else could she possibly be?* Miranda glared at her father's girlfriend, wishing that the woman would just disappear.

The rest of the evening was uneventful. After dinner Miranda headed straight for her room and closed the door behind her.

* * *

"Mom," Miranda began, flipping her long blonde hair through her fingers. "Do you ever go out?" She propped a pillow behind her head as she lay on the couch.

"Go out?" He mom squinted at her from behind the book she was reading. "Well, sure. I go out with my friend Tammy, and your Aunt Tara..."

Miranda shook her head. "No, I mean like dating."

Her mother slid a bookmark in her book and placed it on the coffee table beside her.

"Oh, I see. No, not in quite a while, honey." Smiling, her mom sat up on the couch. "Now if you have any questions..."

"Oh, Mom, no! That's not what I meant." *No way.*

"Oh? Are you sure?" Her mother's eyes sparkled with mischief. If she thought they were going to have a little talk about dating, Miranda needed to set her straight.

"Mom, no. I'm just wondering if you're happy, that's all."

"Oh, I see. Now that your dad has a serious girlfriend, you're wondering about me."

"Serious"? How did Mom even know about this?

"Do you really think that they're serious?" Miranda wanted to know. She had hoped that Sarah was just a passing phase.

"Yes, I do. Your father called me and told me about her a while back. He wanted to ask me how you would best handle it, how to introduce the two of you," her mother stated calmly.

"Doesn't that bother you? I mean, that this Sarah just comes along—"

"No, Miranda, it doesn't," her mother interrupted. "I have nothing against the woman, and neither should you. Your father and I have experienced many problems and Sarah has nothing to do with it. Sarah or no Sarah, your dad and I would never get back together. We just don't work together."

"Oh." Miranda realized suddenly that she had been subconsciously protecting her mother by shutting Sarah out, and wondered if she had been a bit harsh with her dad's girlfriend. But still…

"I know it's difficult for you to see them together," her mother went on. "I'm sure it hurts."

Shaking her head, Miranda spoke up. "It doesn't hurt. I just don't like her. Why do I even have to go over there anymore? You don't make David," she pouted.

"David is eighteen years old. It does bother you, I know it. Besides, your father called me last night."

"She had no business looking at my phone! She deserves everything she gets." Punching the couch pillow, Miranda looked out the window, tears threatening.

"You know that's not fair. Don't you want your father to be happy?" her mother asked.

"How can you say that, after everything that happened?" Miranda's eyes were wide.

"Sometimes in order to be happy yourself, you just have to let things go. Sarah was not that other woman."

How did she know I was aware of the other woman?

"Mom…" Miranda spluttered.

"I knew that you overheard that night. I popped into your bedroom when I heard you crying. I'm so sorry."

"I remember that," Miranda said. "I was so upset with both of you."

"I know. That's when I made the appointment for you to speak with Sherry." Sherry was her therapist from a few years back.

Miranda sat, eyes glued on the bay window.

"Honey. Just give her a chance, let it go."

Her mother's words echoed in her head even after she had walked out of the room. *I don't think I can do that. I'm not as forgiving as you.*

* * *

The dreams were just out of reach, and they were coming more frequently lately. They had been following her since she was a small child. There were variations, but they all involved the ocean and a beautiful blonde woman with crystal blue-green eyes who sucked her in, hypnotized her. This woman's presence wasn't menacing—quite the contrary. She seemed kind, caring, but always out of reach.

This time, the woman's mouth formed words, unspoken words. Trying to lip-read what the woman was saying, Miranda just became more and more frustrated.

Miranda woke with a start, covered in sweat. Her heart was racing as she struggled to catch her breath. She was always curious about these dreams, but *this* one almost felt as if she were so close to solving the mystery of these recurring dreams. She was so very close to finding out what this woman was trying to tell her. The beautiful woman seemed so familiar, like a stunning guardian angel.

Chapter Three

Five months later…

"This trip is going to be just what you need, honey." Miranda's mother threw the last of their bags into the trunk and shut the hatchback with a slam. Then she circled around the car and threw herself into the driver's seat with a sigh as she gathered her straight blonde hair into a ponytail.

It was their annual trip to the Jersey Shore. The shore points of New Jersey were only a few hours from their home in the New York suburbs, so it was easy enough to pack up each year and enjoy the beach and the boardwalk.

"Did you hear me?" Her mother turned in her seat to face Miranda.

Rolling her eyes, Miranda removed her ear buds. "What?"

"I said, this is just what you need."

Looking back and forth between her mother and Eve, Miranda shook her head. "Really?" *Why doesn't Mom understand not to talk about personal things in front of my friends? Geez, how many times do we need to have that conversation?*

"Oops, sorry." Her mother glanced at Eve, who was preoccupied with a game on her phone. Popping her ear buds back into her ears, Miranda tapped her hands on the seat in front of her to the beat of the song.

Miranda couldn't believe that her mom was letting David stay back home with his friend's family. He claimed that he couldn't get off from work at the local mall, where he stocked shelves at one of the electronic stores. She supposed it wouldn't be a fun trip for him anyway, with a bunch of girls.

Her mother did have a point—it had been a rough couple of months. She needed to get her mind off her troubles. School had been challenging this year, with her English honor class putting additional stress on her studies. Still, she ended up completing the year with excellent grades. It looked as if she would continue English honors next year in high school as well.

High school, ugh. That was another stress that plagued her mind lately. With her fourteenth birthday coming up this week, she would be a ninth grader in the fall at Sterling Point High. Glancing over at her best friend eased some anxiety. The two girls had been inseparable since they were three years old. Miranda figured that she should probably lay off the dramatic shows she had been watching in which the best friends fight over boys and part ways.

"It's going to be awesome." Eve grinned widely. Miranda had absolutely no idea what her friend was talking about.

"What?"

"Your birthday! Haven't you been listening?" Eve laughed loudly while pushing her thigh.

"Oh, yeah, it should be fun."

"So I figured we could go to the boardwalk, go on some rides and then come home and we'll open your gift from me." Eve's face lit up.

"Girls, don't forget, we're going out to celebrate! We'll go wherever Miranda wants for dinner, we'll have cake..." her mother declared from the front seat.

Mm. Miranda knew just where she wanted to go for dinner. "Can we go to Antonio's?"

"Of course, birthday girl," her mom answered.

Popping the buds back in her ears, Miranda let the beat of the music soothe her, take her away to another place. Eve had mentioned a gift and seemed very secretive about it. She wondered what her friend had in store for her. One year she had bought Miranda the coolest pair of pajamas from her favorite clothing chain. That was pretty cool—she could use some more pajamas, especially for sleepovers.

Miranda had been so out of sorts lately with the news of her father's engagement last month. She could hardly believe that he was going to marry Sarah. She didn't hide her disappointment when the happy couple had shared the news that day back at her dad's house. Dad had been angry and so had Little Miss Perfect. Miranda wasn't rude or anything; she just kept quiet so that she didn't say something she would regret. What was the problem with that?

Now there was no way on Earth that she could ever move in with her dad. Sarah had been trying really hard to act nice, kind of like a big sister, but Miranda didn't need the woman in her life. She wanted her dad all to herself and, well, Sarah was ruining everything.

She had grown quite distant from her dad over the past few months, refusing to visit his house on weekends. It was killing Miranda to see her relationship with her father deteriorate, but it seemed that he had chosen Sarah's happiness over her own.

The smell of the ocean perked Miranda up as she straightened and glanced out the window. She recognized this area and knew that they were almost at their motel. Miranda recalled past years down by the ocean with both her parents. Eve had usually been there as well.

Miranda glanced at her mom, driving with a pair of big sunglasses on, humming away to the radio. *Poor Mom*, Miranda thought. *Not that I would enjoy having a stepfather, but at least Mom should be out there dating and having some fun, too.*

"Here we are, girls." Her mom pulled into the motel parking lot by the end of the strip of larger motels. This was the place they had stayed for the last several years. It was small, but had a decent pool and clean rooms. "Everybody grab some bags."

Her mother walked to the back of the car to open the hatchback. Miranda unbuckled her seatbelt and adjusted her sunglasses.

"Yes! We are ready to hit the beach, girl!" Eve shouted dramatically.

"Hold on, you two. Help carry these bags in and we can all go down to the beach together." Miranda's mom held out two duffel bags and some small plastic bags.

"Aw, Mom. Come on, we'll be fine. The beach is right across the street," Miranda whined.

"No way. Besides, I'd like to go for a swim as well. We need to check in and get our beach tags for the week."

Shrugging at her friend, Miranda grabbed a bag and followed her mom to the front office. An elderly woman checked them in and gave them two sets of keys for the room. It looked as if they would all share a large room with two queen-sized beds.

"I thought we were getting an adjoining room, Mom." Miranda was annoyed. She and Eve were certainly old enough to be trusted right next door.

"Are you crazy?" her mother exclaimed. "When you have money to buy another room for each night, then you can foot the bill."

"It was worth a shot," Eve smirked as she shrugged her shoulders. Miranda's mom led the way to their room on the first level, right near the pool.

After everyone unpacked their bags, the three changed into their swimsuits and coated themselves in sunblock. In a few minutes, everyone was ready to go.

"You see that?" Miranda's mom said. "I told you it was a good idea to leave early. We practically have the whole day ahead of us."

She was right. The whole day loomed ahead of them and Miranda planned on making it a spectacular one. Looking out at the beach in the midday sun, she felt a wave of something pass through her that she couldn't quite identify. This beach was so familiar to her—not just because she had been coming here since she was a small child, but because she had seen it in her dreams, over and over again. She was sure the rocky shore, and even the lighthouse in the distance, were part of the exact scene she had been witnessing lately in her dreams.

They hit the beach. Eve raced ahead.

"Come on it, the water's beautiful!" she called from the water. Miranda looked back at her mom, who was spreading out the blanket. She stood silent for a moment, concentrating on the feel of the breeze tickling her face.

Then Miranda raced into the surf and dove headfirst into a wave as a delightful sensation of freedom passed through her. She was happy here. She had always been happy here at the beach, in the water. The two girls stayed in the ocean for hours before finally coming out.

"Wow. I was beginning to wonder if the two of you grew fins and were going to take off," her mom chuckled, looking up from her book as the two approached the blanket. *If only,* Miranda thought. *Wouldn't it be great to just swim off toward the horizon, away from school, Dad, Sarah...*

Miranda's mom informed the girls that they would have to leave soon and shower to get ready for dinner. Dinner tonight wouldn't be at Miranda's favorite restaurant, but she was hungry. Wednesday was her birthday and she couldn't wait for Antonio's amazing ravioli. Her mouth practically watered just thinking about it.

"Can we have just a half an hour to walk on the boardwalk, Mom, please?" Miranda attempted to look adorable, her eyes wide, a pleading smile plastered on her face. The boardwalk only boasted a few shops and was mostly occupied by families at this time of day.

"Only if you promise to get me some fudge and taffy at Mariah's." Her mom pulled out her wallet and handed Miranda several bills. "And keep your phone on you. I want you back here in exactly thirty minutes."

"Thanks, Mom!"

The girls took off together, running up the wooden plank to the boardwalk.

"Your mom is so cool," Eve gushed.

"I guess so." Miranda knew that her mom was okay, but she was reluctant to admit it to her friend. "Come on, I'll race you to Mariah's." Miranda took off, feeling more carefree than she had in months.

* * *

Dinner was spaghetti at the Cape Diner. The diner was crowded with tourists, even at eight o'clock when they finally arrived. Miranda's mom had promised to take the girls to the outdoor mall after dinner for some ice cream and souvenir shopping.

Miranda felt the kiss of the sun still warming her cheeks all of these hours later. Why couldn't life be like this all the time? Who needed cold, snowy winters and finals? Who needed a stepmother?

Eve and Miranda had talked for hours at a time about the stepmother problem, and despite joking about ridiculous ways to get rid of her, Miranda knew that she was stuck in a lousy situation. Sure, Sarah was great now, but if it was anything like in the movies, before long Sarah would be taking over the house, bossing her around, and stealing all of her private time with her father. It hurt to see her dad with his arms wrapped around that woman all the time, something that Miranda had rarely witnessed between her parents when she was young. Most of the time, heavy silence had filled the air.

"Honey? Are you okay?" Miranda's mom called out as they made their way toward the pedestrian mall.

"Sure." Glancing at Eve, she saw that her friend was engrossed in her phone. More and more lately, Miranda had been noticing that while she was hanging out with Eve, her friend was busy texting other friends. She considered it rude, but held her tongue.

At the mall, Eve finally looked up from her phone. "What do you say we get ice cream first?" she exclaimed.

"Sounds like a great idea to me." Miranda's mom headed toward the ice cream parlor, which was starting to get crowded.

"Nobody seems to care what I think," grumbled Miranda under her breath.

"What was that, dear?"

"Nothing, Mom. I'm not hungry yet, we just finished dinner, but who cares what I think, anyway?"

"Wow. Somebody has a gigantic attitude," Eve sighed.

"Forget it. We'll get ice cream now. Seems I'm overruled anyway," Miranda muttered. Sure enough, her mom and Eve joined the line now winding around the outdoor patio.

Eve and Miranda's mom were chatting away, laughing and having a grand old time. Miranda stewed through the length of the line. After what seemed like an eternity, they got their orders and decided to window-shop while eating their cones.

"What's the problem now?" Eve inquired, her eyes narrowing at Miranda's scowl.

"Nothing. I'm just not in a good mood," Miranda said through clenched teeth.

"You'd better get over yourself. We have a birthday celebration coming up soon." Eve reminded her.

That brightened Miranda's dark mood for the moment. She had always loved celebrating her summer birthday and this year was no different. Wondering what surprises were in store for her this year, she heard her phone chirp, signaling a new text coming through. It was Stephanie wishing her an early happy birthday. She responded, realizing she might be doing the same rude thing she had mentally accused Eve of doing. Well, even so, she wasn't constantly on her phone.

"Speaking of my birthday, we should try to sneak out to the beach after my mom goes to bed. I've always wanted to go to the beach at night." Usually Miranda followed each and every rule that her mother dished out, but would it hurt her and Eve to sit on the sand in the moonlight and just talk?

"Are you crazy? No way." Eve wasn't one to defy Miranda's mom.

"Party pooper. It's my birthday, let's live a little."

Miranda's mom had just finished looking at a dress on display in one of the shop windows. She caught up with the girls. "Ready to head home soon?"

Yawning into her hand, Miranda couldn't deny the fact that she was beat. "I think that's probably a good idea."

They made their way back to the hotel, walking the few blocks back to their motel.

* * *

The first few days of vacation had passed and Miranda couldn't shake the undeniable feeling that she was missing something, or perhaps missing out on something. Was it normal to feel like this? Irritated, grumpy, sensitive? Was this the fault of all of those teenage hormones that her mom was always talking about lately? Or was she building up her birthday just to be let down by certain disappointment?

The big day was here and Miranda was trying to be a trooper, but both her mom and Eve had been getting on her nerves ever since Sarah had called to ask if she wanted to be a bridesmaid at his wedding.

Was the woman serious? In what world would I want to answer that question, especially on my fourteenth birthday?

Miranda had minded her manners and asked to speak with her father, then blurted out that she wouldn't even be attending, let alone participating in the ceremony. Miranda's mom had snatched the phone away from her, scolding her and apologizing to her dad. Couldn't everyone just leave her alone and let her enjoy her birthday? And what was up with her mother, acting like she was okay with her father just up and marrying another woman? Why didn't all of the grown-ups in her life just grow up already?

"Cheer up, it's your day." Eve glanced at Miranda, shaking her head.

"Oh, okay. Tell me, exactly how happy would you be if the wicked witch called *you* on *your* birthday and asked you to be in her wedding?" Miranda waited for a response.

"Well, I guess if you put it that way…"

"Exactly," Miranda muttered. Feeling the warm sand on her feet, she gazed out at the ocean, her rattled thoughts momentarily soothed. Nobody seemed to understand how she felt. Nobody in this entire world *got* her. It was unbelievable.

Eve squinted in the sun, also gazing out at the horizon, her brown curly hair sweeping her eyes. "You ready to head back and shower before dinner?"

"Sure, let's go," Miranda huffed.

Brushing the sand off her thighs, Eve rose and offered Miranda a hand getting up.

Chapter Four

Antonio's didn't disappoint. The ravioli was delicious, and Miranda actually felt herself relax during her birthday dinner. Miranda's mom had even arranged for the waiter to bring over a slice of cake with a candle on it for her birthday. Not only did the waiter, her mom, and Eve sing to her, but it seemed the entire restaurant joined in as well. Although secretly thrilled, Miranda acted embarrassed when the spotlight was on her.

Round two of the birthday celebration took place back at the motel, with a chocolate-chip cookie cake and presents from her mom. Eve had been secretive, stating that she wished to give Miranda her present later, in private.

"In private?" Miranda's mom scrunched her brows. "Where do you guys think we are? This is a motel room, and I'm here for the night."

"Mrs. James," Eve began. "Could we just go across the street and sit on the beach for a while? It's not even dark yet, and it *is* Miranda's fourteenth birthday, after all."

"I'm quite aware of Miranda's age, Eve. What would be the problem with me joining you guys?"

"Mom, come on. I'm not a baby. Could you please stop being so overprotective? Don't you trust me?" Miranda winced as she heard the whining tone of her own voice. She gazed into her mother's blue eyes, a shade lighter than her own.

"It's not you I don't trust. It's the other people." Miranda's mom had been telling her this for years now.

"I'll bring my phone. We'll be back in half an hour—forty-five minutes, tops," Miranda pleaded.

Throwing her hands up, Miranda's mom acquiesced. "Okay, okay. But half an hour, that's it—and call me if there are any suspicious-looking people."

"Thanks, Mom!" Springing to her feet, Miranda embraced her mom, who shook her head and muttered something unintelligible.

"Whew! Let this party begin!" Eve rushed over to the small wooden table in the corner of the room and grabbed a large, rectangular package. Then she trotted to the door, holding it open for Miranda.

"Bye, Mom!" Miranda exclaimed.

"Hold on. Give me a hug, birthday girl." Miranda cringed, though deep down she reveled in being her mom's little girl. Chuckling, Eve skipped out the door, heading down the pathway to the street.

Since the beach was directly across the street, the girls found themselves sitting on the sand in no time.

"So what's the big secret?" Miranda asked.

"Open it!" Eve squealed, holding her hands over her mouth in delight.

With her eyes wide, Miranda tore through the package and gasped as she saw finally what the gift was.

"Thank you!" she gushed, turning the box over in her hands to examine the print. It was the game she had wanted—though her mom didn't make a secret of the fact that she thought it was garbage.

Spellbound had been around for some time. Even Miranda's mom claimed to have played it when she was a teenager. The game promised magic, mystery, and fun. A series of spaces marked the board and when you rolled the dice, you had to follow the directions on the designated spot. A group of Miranda's friends had played it once at a sleepover at Stephanie's house. Miranda had landed on a spot that had asked her to conjure up a mythical creature. Her chant for a beautiful fairy hadn't succeeded, but it was tons of fun nonetheless.

"No wonder you wanted to give this to me out here. Mom would flip." Miranda giggled as the wind slowly picked up speed.

"Is it supposed to storm tonight?" Eve spun her head around, taking in the vast beach.

"I think so, a little bit later. We should get started or Mom will come find us if we're late." Glancing back toward the motel, Miranda rubbed her hands together. "Let's do this." She opened the package, tossing the plastic and gift wrap in the nearby trash can.

"I hope I get to dare you to do anything I want," Eve squealed, throwing her head back in laughter.

"Wrong game. This is not Truth or Dare." Miranda knew that a spot on the board allowed you to command a game member to do anything, but that was *not* going to happen. She would rather walk away than let Eve embarrass her.

Sure enough, after about ten minutes of playing the game, Eve landed on her favorite spot. Miranda could feel a wave of tension seep through her body as she witnessed Eve scanning the beach. *No, there was no way that she would actually expect me to...*

"Got it!" Eve leaned closer to Miranda, squirming. "See that guy playing ball, the one with the blue shorts and dark hair?" *Was she kidding? Of course Eve would zero in on the group of boys playing football.*

Rising to her feet, Miranda swept the sand off her shorts. "No way! It's almost time to go back anyway." Miranda secretly willed her mother to come out to the beach to get them. No such luck. It figured that this would be one of the times that her mom would leave her alone.

"You have to, it's in the rules." Eve chided, standing now, glancing at the boys with her hand placed on her hip. "Besides, you don't even know what I'm going to ask you to do."

"Fine. What are you asking me to do?"

A grin a mile wide formed on Eve's face. "Ask that guy if he would like to come over and sing 'Happy Birthday' to you."

Crossing her arms in front of her chest, Miranda stood her ground. "No."

"I see. Well, if I remember correctly, this is a dare and if you don't follow through, there will be consequences." Eve examined her fingernails as if she didn't have a care in the world.

Red heat crept up Miranda's face. She could practically feel her blood boiling. "Eve, I swear, if you do anything..."

"Do it. Now," Eve challenged.

"No," Miranda retorted.

Shaking her head, Eve headed toward the group of boys. Was she seriously going to do this? "Eve! Wait!"

Spinning her head around, Eve stopped in the sand. "Go ahead."

There was no way on Earth that she could ever ask that boy to sing her "Happy Birthday"—no way! Whatever Eve had up her sleeve couldn't be worse than that. "I'm going back to the room."

"Hey, do you guys want another player? My friend has been watching, afraid to ask," Eve called over the boys. Miranda stood, frozen to the spot, her heart racing.

Laughter filled the air as the boys stood, assessing her. The tallest boy spoke first. "I'm pretty sure that neither of you would know a thing about how to play football."

"Yeah, let's play a game, and it's *not* touch football," a blond boy shouted, sticking out his chest.

The boy in the blue shorts stood silently. He poked his blond friend and leaned over to whisper something in his ear. The shouting stopped. Miranda was helpless to do anything but stare.

"Oh, yeah! I know plenty about football!" Eve shouted as the boys gathered up their football and continued playing.

The dark-haired boy turned to gaze at Miranda. In the fading light, it was difficult to make out his features, but he appeared to be quite handsome. Miranda broke the stare first, turning back to face her friend. Eve was doubled over in huge gasps of laughter. Bending down to snatch her bag, Miranda stomped off.

"Hey! Stop! Don't be such a wet blanket, come on!" Eve caught up with her and grabbed her by the elbow. "It's your birthday, lighten up!"

"Get off me! I'm not speaking to you!"

They advanced up the sandy path to the street. Eve spoke again.

"Did you see the way the guy in the blue shorts was looking at you?"

That stopped Miranda in her tracks. He had looked back and she couldn't help but notice how cute he was. "No." Her head dropped.

Taking her hand, Eve led her back to the spot in the sand where the game lay, unfinished. "Let's just finish the game. Don't be mad."

"I guess." Part of the reason that she was friends with Eve was because of the fact that she was so outgoing and brazen, fun to be around.

"Sit." Eve sat first, pulling Miranda down to join her. The sky was darkening, the clouds threatening rain. Miranda swept a hand over her face to keep the wind from blowing her hair in her eyes.

"It's past a half an hour. We should probably get back." Something about the dark clouds overhead caused her to worry.

"You take one more turn, then we'll go." Eve crossed her legs in the sand.

"I don't know, it looks like it's going to downpour at any minute." Glancing at the ocean, Miranda felt a chill race up her spine as the waves crashed into the rocks.

"One more turn." Eve's eyes were wide with mischief.

"Okay, let's get this over with and then we'll head back." Miranda couldn't believe that her mom wasn't calling them back yet.

She rolled the dice and it landed with a thud. Six spaces. *One, two, three, four, five, six.* She secured her shiny game piece on the board.

Glancing down to read the spot, Miranda shrieked. It was the spot she had been waiting for.

The sound of the wind beckoned in her ear, the crashing of the waves all around.

"What are you going to conjure up?" Eve rubbed her palms together, squinting at Miranda.

The roar of the waves increased, and the wind intensified. It was suddenly darker. The beach took on another form, exactly as it had been in all of her dreams: the rocks, the shore, it all looked so surreal. Glancing around, Miranda saw the dark-haired boy approaching, his shadowy figure coming closer.

The sound of her mother's voice filled the air. Miranda spun around to see her advancing upon them from the street.

"If I need you, let it be, if you need me, look to the sea."

The chant whirled out of her mouth. She had no idea where the words had come from. Thunder boomed and lightning crackled as Miranda stood and strode toward the water. She padded on the soft sand as pellets of rain pounded down, the wind kicked up higher, and the ocean roared. Her mind focused on the water.

Then everything went black.

Chapter Five

Cold, black water seeped through her, straight to her bones. Struggling to breathe, Miranda felt a wave crash over her, causing her to lose her footing. Her teeth chattered as she felt another wave crash, pulling her under, deeper, deeper. Recognition washed over her. Of course—it was just like in her dreams. But it was more than a dream. She knew that she had experienced this before, although the water wasn't as dark or as cold as it was now.

How had she survived last time? Did she fight her way up to the surface? Kicking with all of her strength, Miranda held her breath and fought her way up, only to be dragged back down. She was being pulled into deeper water, thrown by the current, helpless to do anything but let the water consume her.

Gulping down seawater, Miranda knew that she was in trouble. With the force of a hammer, it hit her what had happened all those years ago. The image of a beautiful blonde woman appeared before her, reaching for her hand. Her face glowed in the dark water, her crystal blue-green eyes sparkling with warmth.

The moment that Miranda reached for the woman's hand, the moment she made contact, she could breathe. She was going to be okay. Air filled her lungs and she fought the urge to panic, clutching the woman's hand for dear life. Somehow, this woman was her connection to living and she wasn't about to let go.

Gliding through the water effortlessly, Miranda's senses were now on high alert, the colors vivid, the sensation of movement surreal. As odd as it sounded, she had never felt more alive than at this very moment.

After a few minutes of graceful twists and turns through the salty seawater, Miranda wondered where this creature was taking her. Yes, she supposed the woman was a creature. Almost embarrassed to look, she slowly took in the elegant green fins, the shimmering torso and the long, streaming blonde hair.

This creature was a mermaid.

A mermaid! Miranda liked to think that she was a smart, sensible person, but she couldn't deny what was right before her very own eyes. This woman had saved her before, many, many years ago. She had been so very young. Now this woman had somehow been trying to communicate with her through her dreams. *But why? Why me? Why now?*

As if sensing her thoughts, the enchanting creature, woman, whatever she was, spun her head back for the briefest of moments to smile warmly at Miranda. Her heart leapt in her chest. She was almost too stunning to look at.

Beckoning with her finger, the creature glided her way up the surface, releasing her grip on Miranda. Panicking, Miranda reached for her, but the mermaid swam ahead quickly, disappearing from sight. Choking on saltwater now, Miranda knew that she was capable of reaching the surface safely, but feared being left alone in the vast, dark ocean.

Moving as quickly as she could, she held her breath, eyes straining to spot the shimmery fins straight ahead. *There she was!* Miranda was right upon her! She splashed up through the surface of the black water, gasping aloud when she finally broke through.

The air was cold against her skin, a mist of salty spray hitting her again and again. The sky was black and the creature was nowhere to be found. Miranda struggled for breath, treading water. She had despised her childhood swimming lessons, but was grateful now that her mother had insisted upon them.

"Hey! Hey!" Miranda called out. With only the moonlight to guide her, she continued forward, using her arms and legs to hold herself above water. She soon grew tired as the waves, crashing into her, forced her to tread harder. It seemed as if hours had gone by, although Miranda knew that it was probably only minutes. Perhaps her eyes had adjusted to the darkness, as she could make out the tips of a rocky jetty in the water about ten feet away.

A slight giggling sound filled the darkness, a sound so quiet that Miranda may have missed it. Making her way over to the boulders, she spotted the mermaid lying on the largest boulder, sprawled out with her hand cradling her head.

"Hey!" she called out again, climbing up a nearby rock.

"I knew you'd find me." The woman's silken voice washed over her.

"Who are you? Why did you leave me?" Miranda panted, her pulse still racing.

Chuckling softly, the woman patted the vacant spot next to her. "I knew that you'd be full of questions. Sit."

"But what happened here? Where am I?" Miranda's eyes filled with tears at the thought of being so far from her mom and Eve. They must be sick with worry.

"Dear child, take a deep breath and relax."

Miranda sensed that none of her questions would be answered if she didn't do as she was told. Willing herself to breathe slower, she took a moment before speaking. "Okay, please. Tell me."

"You've been worried. A lot of troubles on your mind lately, am I right?" The mermaid batted her long, thick lashes at Miranda.

Gazing down, Miranda placed one trembling hand on top of the other to still them. "Well, I guess." Her voice came out as a mere squeak. Clearing her throat, she peered directly into the creature's eyes.

"I apologize. It seems as if I've been rude. You don't even know my name and here I am just firing off questions to you." This woman/creature/mermaid was certainly odd. Stroking her endless hair, she glanced down at the rock, as if ashamed. There was something innocent about this creature—innocent but worldly at the same time. This creature was like a riddle, one that Miranda wasn't sure if she would ever figure out.

"What...what's your name?" Miranda ventured.

"You must think I'm something, rescuing you and then letting you go just before we reached the surface." Giggling softly, the creature seemed to find it amusing that she had scared her.

Miranda opened her mouth to speak, but was cut off by the mermaid's sweet, drifting voice.

"Sweetheart, part of the test, part of being here, is to see if you're strong enough to survive, make it on your own. In a safe, controlled environment, of course." The creature met her gaze, chuckling.

"Was I?" Miranda wondered aloud. "*Am* I strong enough?"

"Are you here?"

"Of course I'm here." Miranda spread her arms in front of her, motioning that she was very much alive.

"Then, yes, you're strong enough."

"Would you have let me die back there?" Miranda was incredulous. This mermaid was starting to rattle her, speaking in riddles again.

"No, Miranda. Have some faith in me. Of course not." She puffed air from her lip.

Miranda remained silent, knowing that answers would come only when this creature was ready to give them.

"Cat got your tongue?" More laughter.

"Please, stop that! Stop! Tell me, why am I here?" Miranda exclaimed, glancing all around.

"You're not happy, are you? I've been waiting for you to remember, waiting for you to call for me."

"What do you mean? I'm happy enough. I don't understand…"

"You haven't been happy in quite a while, not since before your parents' divorce—and then there's Sarah. Ugh, Sarah." The mermaid twisted her face.

How on earth did this creature know about Sarah, or about any of this? "How did you—"

"I know *everything*. My name is Abigail, in case you don't remember."

"Abigail?" The name sounded familiar, but just out of reach.

"Abby."

"Yes, Abby. I remember now." Crashing waves and bright blonde hair came to mind.

The waxing moon shone above, illuminating Abby's striking beauty. Reaching over to take Miranda's hand, Abby clutched it in her own.

Feeling awkward, Miranda was about to pull away and then hesitated. There was warmth and beauty to her touch.

"Where am I? Please, tell me."

"Miranda, you're where you want to be, where you've been subconsciously asking me to bring you."

But that didn't make any sense. "What do you mean? Am I okay? Can I go back home? My mom, she's got to be worried sick." A sensation not unlike fear crept through Miranda's skin.

"I promise you that you're safe and your mom doesn't even know you're gone."

She doesn't even know that I'm gone? How could that be? Of course my own mother would know that I'm gone.

As if reading her thoughts, Abby tossed an arm around Miranda's shoulder. "All in good time. You'll understand all of this in good time."

Chapter Six

"Where are you taking me?" Miranda asked as Abby grabbed her hand, ready to delve into the deep, dark water once again. Feeling anxious at the thought of returning into those churning waters, Miranda pulled back abruptly.

"Don't worry, I won't let go." Abby winked before pulling them both into the water with a splash.

The chill of the water seemed to disappear as Abby held onto her, and once again, she could breathe just fine. Her senses returned to high alert as Miranda took in the brightly colored fish in the darkened water. The journey took no more than five minutes, as Abby's speed increased considerably. *Exactly how fast could she swim?*

Straight ahead, a dim light grew brighter with each passing second. Abby's tail twitched briskly, as if excited by the upcoming destination. Spinning to face Miranda, the mermaid winked and swam even faster until they reached a series of underwater caves. Swooshing into the largest cave, Miranda clutched Abby's hand tightly, aware that they were probably at least a thousand feet deep. There was no way that she could make it out of this alive if Abby decided to pull another one of her tricks down here. *But why would she?* As kooky as this mermaid was, something deep inside of Miranda told her that Abby would never let any real harm come to her.

Blinding light forced Miranda to shield her eyes as she heard that eerie giggle escape from

Abby's lips. Before them stood a town. Miranda gasped in awe. She had never seen anything quite so beautiful. Shades of blue, green, red, violet, and everything in between made the town appear as if it were lit from within.

Still holding onto her hand, Abby led her to the center of the village where tiny merchildren gathered around a fountain. Male and female creatures swam to and fro, socializing, working, and relaxing. *How odd,* Miranda thought. *It was just like back at home, but more colorful, louder—more everything.* Chatter could be heard throughout the town square. These creatures could speak clearly and be understood quite well under water. Opening her own mouth, she found that the words came easily.

Gazing down at Miranda, Abby ruffled the girl's flowing wet hair. "Yes, you can speak. Just as easily as any of us now." Then she slowly pried her fingers from Miranda's clutching grip. "It's okay," she reassured Miranda, seeing her panicked face. "You're safe down here in our little town. Promise."

Trusting her, Miranda stepped back from Abby, who had quickly become her lifeline in a matter of mere hours. "Wow," was all she could muster.

A small merchild drifted over and pulled on Miranda. Before long a small group of children had clustered around her, staring, their mouths open, touching her gently.

'Um." Miranda glanced at Abby for support.

"It's fine. They're just curious, they won't hurt you." Abby moved in front of her, motioning for the young children to move back. Instantly the children swam backward at least several feet, still oohing and ahhing. "They haven't seen a human before, these really young ones."

"The older ones have, though?" Miranda pointed at the adults, some watching her and others just going about their business.

"Most have, yes." Abby's voice was soothing, gentle, as a small bubble escaped her lips.

"Where did the humans go?" Miranda didn't see any other humans here.

"Well, some have left, gone back, and some are right here in front of you." Abby's arm swirled gracefully through the water.

"I don't see them."

"Remember when I told you that you would understand everything in good time?"

Miranda knew she would have to wait for the answer. "Yes, I know."

"Good. Now come, let's find Elise."

"Elise?"

A young mermaid who appeared to be around Miranda's age came swimming over.

"Did I hear somebody call my name?" Elise's flowing brown hair drifted upward. Her brown eyes peered into Miranda's dark blue ones.

"I think I'll give you girls some time to get acquainted. Now, Elise, play nice," Abby instructed.

"Yes, Mother." Her eyes rolling upward, Elise giggled and took in Miranda standing before her.

One thing that Miranda quickly learned was that you couldn't stand in the depths of the ocean with your mouth hanging open without saltwater gushing in. She gasped for air. Elise placed a hand on her shoulder.

"Relax, breathe," Elise commanded.

"That...she's...your *mother*?" Miranda spluttered.

"Yup." Elise nodded coolly. "That she is."

"She's awesome. I mean, you're so lucky!" Miranda exclaimed.

"Hm, see how you would feel if she was on *your* case every single second." She rolled her eyes again. It seemed that even in this magical town, the classic mother/daughter relationship remained the same.

Scrutinizing Elise, Miranda realized that she looked vaguely familiar. Kind of like Eve, but something about her mannerisms reminded Miranda of herself—the way she moved her hands when she spoke, the tilt of her head. But there was Eve again, in that lopsided grin. It was downright creepy.

"What? What are you staring at?" Elise moved away self-consciously.

"No, it's just that you remind me of someone. My best friend, actually."

"Oh! Is that all?" Elise swam to Miranda's side and took her hand. "Come, I'll show you around."

"Wait. Do you know how long I'll be here for?" If she wasn't going to get a straight answer from Abby, she might as well give her daughter a shot.

Shaking her head from side to side, Elise was adamant. "All in good time, Miranda..."

Finishing the other girl's sentence, Miranda mumbled to herself, "All in good time."

* * *

For hours, she and Elise explored various caves and met other young mermaids and mermen.

One merman had resembled her own father so closely that she had to do a double take. This place was like an alternate universe, it seemed—except that life here appeared to be happier, more carefree. Back at home everyone always appeared to be in a rush, running late to school, work, dance.

Although she had had an unbelievable day, Miranda grew more and more worried about her mother. Why did Abby say that her mother didn't even know she was gone? Why did Abby avoid all of her questions about her return home? It seemed that each time she brought it up today, both Abby and Elise had changed the subject and found something even more amazing to look at.

Miranda caught herself staring at the back of Elise's shoulder blade. Elise had a teeny, tiny birthmark there in the shape of a heart—just like Miranda did.

"What are you looking at?" Elsie moved back slightly.

"Sorry, it's just that you have this birthmark so much like mine." Miranda peeled her hair away from her shoulder so that the girl could see.

"Hmm, that's funny. Maybe it means we're going to be great friends." Elise took her hands in hers and chuckled. There were a lot of unexplainable things down here. Miranda supposed she could just add this to the list.

It had to be in the middle of the night, but nobody appeared to be tired or sleeping. As a matter of fact, Miranda herself felt a surge of energy. She didn't feel tired in the least.

"Do you guys sleep?" Miranda asked Abby.

"No need. We don't sleep because we don't need to. We never tire." She performed an underwater flip.

So they didn't sleep, but did they ever eat? Her stomach was gurgling, having forgotten about eating up until now.

"Do we eat? Do we *eat*? Of course we eat!" Abby burst out laughing. Elise clutched Miranda's hand. "As a matter of fact, we were just sitting down to supper."

Elise guided her into a large, enchanting cave. The inside of the cave was lit in all of the colors of the rainbow. There was a kitchen of sorts, with a small eating area and sink.

"Sit." Elise helped her mother bring dishes of food to the table. Before Miranda appeared the most spectacular-looking meal she had ever seen: fresh vegetables, fish, and warm, soft rolls. Just like her other senses, her sense of taste was heightened. Miranda had never had such a delicious meal before.

After finishing the extraordinary meal, Miranda helped clean the dishes in the large sink. The routine of eating dinner and cleaning the kitchen calmed her, but also reminded her of being back home with her mom and David. Some of Abby's mannerisms were so similar to her mother's. Even her blonde hair and eyes were enough to make Miranda think of her mom.

Abby surprised her with a delicious chocolate birthday cake, dressed up with icing and fourteen candles. How had she known? This mermaid seemed to know everything.

"Go ahead, dear, Give her the gift," Abby instructed, nodding at Elise. Squealing with delight, Elise handed her a small blue box adorned with tiny white shells. Miranda hesitated, recalling that she had just experienced a similar ritual with her own mother and Eve. *I miss them.*

Opening the delicate box, Miranda held her breath. Before her eyes was a sparkling turquoise jewel attached to a brilliant white gold chain. It was simply the most gorgeous thing that Miranda had laid eyes on.

"Thank you, both of you." The gift brought a lump to her throat. Abby and Elise wrapped her in an embrace.

Just that very night, Miranda had received her favorite DVD from her mom. Somehow, as stunning as the necklace was, it wasn't nearly as special to her as the movie.

Miranda's thoughts were consumed by her mother and home when Abby told Elise that she needed a private moment with Miranda. Elise glanced back forth at the two before heading into another section of the underwater home.

"Sit," Abby ordered, pulling a small chair out for Miranda. She obeyed. "I want you to have an open mind, to let go of your worry."

"But I can't if I have no idea what's happened here," Miranda said, throwing up her arms in frustration.

"Miranda. Try to have some fun, forget about your home for a few days." Abby reached for her shoulder.

"I want to go home." She wasn't sure until that very moment, but now she felt strongly that she should get back. She had had her fun and now it was time to leave.

"You're not ready. That's all I can say. It would be in your best interest to just relax and enjoy yourself," Abby soothed.

"But you just can't keep me here and not tell me where I am, why my own mother isn't even worried about me..." Tears escaped, blending with the saltwater.

"Honey, believe it or not, I have nothing but your best interests at heart. Your mother isn't worried because she doesn't know. Besides, haven't you been complaining how lame your mother is and all of that?" *How does she know this? Does this creature have the ability to read my mind?* Frustration boiled in her blood as Miranda clenched both of her hands into tight fists.

"She doesn't *know?* You don't make any sense! I'll just leave myself then!" Tossing the necklace on the table, she took off without thinking. Swimming toward the exit of the cave, Miranda heard Abby call after her, but she was so furious that she kept moving. She heard Elise close behind, calling out her name, and yelled back for everyone to leave her alone. It wasn't far now to the mouth of the cave—this tiny town of sorts was easy enough to navigate.

Miranda hesitated but plowed on, feeling braver than she had since this whole adventure had begun. Darkness and cold were up ahead. Miranda could sense it before she came upon it.

Whoosh! Powering through, she gulped huge quantities of saltwater. The exit into the ocean was worse than she had imagined. Perhaps it was because she was so deep, or perhaps it had to do with the magic of the mermaid town, but she found that she couldn't breathe, even for a minute—and worse, she could no longer hold her breath. She was horrified. *What was this place?*

In a panic, Miranda turned blindly back toward the cave, but instead slammed hard into an invisible wall. Her breaths came in rasps, sucking in more saltwater. Flinging herself at the invisible wall, she saw Elise rushing to help her.

A sucking vortex pulled her into the town with such force that it felt like the wind had been knocked out of her. Elise's face registered compassion and empathy.

"Please, listen to my mom. Forget about getting out of here for now. You can't, you won't. It's impossible until you're ready."

Chapter Seven

To the best of her knowledge, it had been at least a week since she had arrived on her birthday evening, although it was hard to tell because nobody slept around here. It felt like years, though the knowledge that her family didn't know that she was gone calmed her. After days of resisting, pouting, and throwing grown-up temper tantrums, Miranda resigned herself to the fact that she might as well stop fighting this.

In the meantime, she resolved to have fun and enjoy her relationship with Abby and her newfound friendship with Elise. Elise was quite possibly the coolest friend a girl could ask for. She allowed Miranda to choose the games they played without pressuring her to play Truth or Dare. She wasn't constantly on her phone, although to be fair, there were no cell phones down here. Abby was a good mother figure, but also tried to be her friend, giving into her every wish—except one, that is.

"I want you to meet someone," Elise announced one day, a smug grin plastered to her face.

"Oh no, what are you up to?" Miranda cringed. She had seen that look before, on both Eve and Elise.

"Trust me. Pinky promise." They locked pinkies, and Miranda felt herself lightening up. The girls were getting pretty tight, with their own signals and hand gestures. Truth be told, Elise was becoming like a sister to her. David was a cool older brother and everything, but there was nothing like having a sister to share all of your secrets with.

Elise dragged her out of their cave and into the brighter community outside. Miranda spied two young mermen approaching. One was fair, like herself, and the other was quite handsome, with dark hair and piercing gray eyes. The blond had eyes for Elise. He swam right up to Elise and drew her into an embrace. Miranda glanced at them and then quickly averted her eyes to the sandy bottom.

"Miranda, I'd like you to meet Thomas and Evan." The teenagers nodded in her direction.

"Pleased to meet you." Miranda felt red heat crawl up her cheeks as she noticed Evan, the darker one, eying her legs.

Knowing that he had been caught, Evan blushed himself. "Ah, sorry. It's not too often that a human graces us with their presence. Welcome." Reaching over, he extended his hand, a goofy grin playing on his lips. Goofy, but kind of adorable.

Thomas swam over and embraced her. "Any sister of Elise's is welcome here." The forceful hug startled her, causing her to lose her footing. Thomas helped her up, this time standing back a bit.

"Oh, well, I'm not her sister, but thanks."

"Yes, around here you are, and considering she's my girl, that makes you like family."

Oh. She hadn't expected that. Everybody in this town was beyond friendly and inviting. *Why couldn't humans behave so respectfully and peacefully all the time?* She figured they could learn a thing or two from these hospitable creatures.

"Well, okay then. Thank you."

"Come, on, let's get out of this place and have some fun." Evan grabbed her hand and started for the exit cave.

"Oh, no. I can't. You see—"

Giggling not unlike her mother, Elise spun around and poked Miranda in the belly. "You'll be fine, silly. As long as you hold Evan's hand tightly." Elise winked at Evan, causing Miranda to blush again.

"I promise I will not let anything happen to you. Trust me?" Evan peered at Miranda through gray hooded eyes. The warmth of his smile heated her body. What choice did she have but to follow him? She held on tightly and pressed her eyes shut.

They burst through the exit of the little village.

"Whew!" Thomas cheered, holding Elise's hand and placing a brief kiss on her forehead.

"Where are we going?" Miranda glanced around, a sudden fear of sharks building up in her mind.

"There's no sharks down here. Besides, they don't bother with us," Elise said.

"How did you know what I was thinking?" Miranda blurted.

"I inherited the ability from my mom." She shrugged her shoulders and swam on. *Great, now I live with two people—scratch that, two creatures—who can read my mind at any given time.*

The path to their destination was filled with odd, colorful animals of all shapes and sizes. A giant orca whale swept up to them, stopping to scoop Elsie onto its back. Squealing with delight, Miranda clapped her hands, wishing she had a video camera to capture the moment.

"Come, Evan, bring her closer." With a swish, Evan handed Miranda over to Elise, who lifted her onto the whale's back. "Hold onto me tight. Don't let go."

The sensation was out of this world. It was like being in a race car speeding through the ocean. Miranda recalled the time she had been horseback riding at the beach with her dad. It was exhilarating, like she was flying. She turned back to face Evan and he flashed a grin, giving her a big thumbs-up.

Before long, the whale gently bounced the girls off and lunged ahead through the crystal blue water.

"That. Was. Amazing." Miranda hugged Elise with a tiny squeal and drifted back to Evan, who was ready to grab her.

"You're a natural." Evan's eyes lit up, taking her in.

Suddenly shy, Miranda dropped her gaze but clutched his hand tighter as they continued on. Miranda had exactly zero experience with boys and the attention that Evan was paying her stirred up mixed emotions. On one hand, she was attracted to him, pleased that he was showering her with attention. On the other hand, she was unsure of herself, nervous about what to say and how to act. Clearing her throat, she decided to just go with the feeling, swearing never to forget this moment as long as she lived.

Their destination drawing closer, a green tint spread over the ocean floor. Watching in amazement, Miranda and Evan followed Elise and Thomas into a sort of field, dotted with bright, phosphorescent plants. Miranda opened her mouth to speak but no words would come. Evan placed her down on the floor and nodded at the other couple, who took off in the opposite direction.

"Where are you guys going?" Miranda felt her heart race at the thought of being left alone with Evan.

"We'll be back soon, promise." Sticking her pinky out in the glowing water, Elise flipped gracefully and led the way onward, with Thomas following.

"Let's sit for a while. This is my favorite place. I come here when I want to be alone and think." Evan was gazing down at the brightly lit floor. She felt privileged to have been brought here, to Evan's special place.

Not wanting to interrupt his thoughts, Miranda waited in silence until he spun to face her, his face lighting up.

"I'm so happy to have you here, to share this with you." His voice was soft, but deep. Eve would never believe in a million years that she was sitting on a phosphorescent floor in the deep ocean with the most handsome boy she had ever seen.

Evan reached over to take her hand. Her heart must have stopped beating for a moment, because she couldn't breathe, couldn't think. Her senses were on high alert.

"Tell me about yourself." Evan held onto her hand as he looked deeply into her eyes. His gray irises unsettled her. He was simply amazing.

"Me?" *Duh, of course he's asking me, who else is here?* Feeling the warmth in her cheeks, she cleared her throat and told this handsome young man about her life back home.

Listening intently, he spoke only when she had finished. "It seems to me that you have a very happy life back home."

"You seem surprised. Did you expect that it would be awful?" Miranda scrunched her brows.

"Not awful, I guess. But I figured you came here for a reason. Most of you do." *Most of us? Exactly what did that mean?*

"I don't understand. You mean humans?" A bright pink fish flitted by, tickling Miranda with its fins.

"Don't you know? You were brought here for a reason. The reason—well, you have to figure that out." He peered into her eyes, running a thumb along the outside of her hand.

That gave Miranda pause. She *had* been doing an awful lot of complaining lately, what with her father getting remarried, her mother on her case, Eve irritating her. But wasn't all of this considered normal? Teenagers complained, right? Why was she brought here?

Eve's face came to mind, telling her that she had a major attitude. Her mom reprimanding her to clean her room over and over. Her dad lecturing her once again to be kind to Sarah. Maybe it was all too much to take.

"This is beautiful. Did Abby and Elise give this to you?" Evan fingered the bright jewel around her neck, which was now glowing in the light.

His mere touch startled her, causing her to catch her breath. Finding her voice, she answered. "Yes, how did you know?"

"This type of beauty only comes from the sea." It was true. She was pretty confident that nothing like this existed in her own world. "It's beautiful."

He lifted her chin and she knew in her heart what was coming next. Holding her breath, she leaned into him as he moved to touch his lips to hers.

The sensation was unbelievable, as sparks of electricity consumed her. Evan's kiss was soft and sweet. She had imagined many times what it would be like to kiss a boy, embarrassed to think she had even practiced on her own hand. But this? Never in her wildest dreams could she ever have imagined this.

"Wow." Evan released her and sat back, still holding her hand. "That was *amazing*." Miranda knew that Evan needed to hold her hand to keep her breathing, but at that moment it felt like more.

Miranda figured that a boy like Evan had probably had a lot more experience than she did when it came to matters like kissing.

"Only one other time." He gazed into her dark blue eyes.

"Oh. Oh, no, don't tell me that you can read minds, too." She was mortified.

Chuckling softly, he shook his head. "No, not me. I just saw the look on your face and figured that you might be thinking about me here, with lots of mermaids."

"Whew. That's a relief." Miranda let out a sight. "But, come on. Look around at all of these beautiful mermaids. You surely must have had girlfriends by your age."

"Miranda, I'm only turning sixteen in a few months. There's only been one other girl." His gray eyes dropped to the ground.

Miranda felt herself deflate momentarily. "What...what happened? Where is she?"

Glancing around the beautiful field of glowing fish and plants, he steadied himself before answering. "She's gone."

"Gone? But where?" Miranda couldn't imagine that she would have gotten too far around here.

The look on his face spoke volumes. Suddenly she figured it out. Her jaw dropped and she clamped her mouth down on the words that threatened to escape.

"Now it seems that you're the mind reader." Evan smoothed her blonde hair away from her face.

"She left?" Miranda squeaked.

"Yup, but it's okay. That was a while ago."

"It couldn't have been that long ago. I'm sorry."

Rubbing her hand, he pulled her up to face him. "Let's go find Elise and Thomas."

Was he upset with her? She shouldn't have asked about the girl. As if sensing her worry, Evan leaned down to kiss her lightly on her forehead. "No worries, huh?"

"No worries." Miranda swam alongside him, holding onto his hand, enjoying the strange, mystical surroundings. There were creatures down here that she had never imagined were possible. Boy, her science teacher, Mr. Hilt, would have a field day down here.

Elise and Thomas were in their sights up ahead. Coming straight for them, Elise wore a grin a mile wide. She grabbed her by the arm.

"Hey!"

Miranda winced.

"Evan, I'll have her back in no time." Elise pulled Miranda away from the boys, further and further until they reached a secluded spot near a small cave.

"Tell me *everything!*" Elise demanded, turning somersaults in the water and dragging Miranda right along with her.

"Oh, it was nothing." Miranda tried her hand at playing it cool, throwing her shoulders up in a shrug.

"Nothing? Spill it. I can read your mind, remember?"

Miranda tried desperately to push all thoughts of Evan out of her mind, knowing that she had failed miserably.

"Oh, okay. It was spectacular! It was amazing! It was…" Miranda was at a loss for words. Elise pulled her friend in for a hug.

"He really likes you, you know." Elise was serious now. Miranda realized with a start that Elise could read the minds of other mermaids and mermen, too.

"He does?" Miranda bit her lip.

"Yes, and don't worry about Justine."

"Justine?" This mind-reading business was unnerving.

"Yes, his old girlfriend."

"Was he serious about her?" she ventured, fidgeting from one foot to the next.

"Justine was a girl he was starting to like. She liked him too, but apparently not quite enough."

"What do you mean?"

"She chose to go back to her old life." Elise covered her mouth as if realizing that she had said too much—a gesture Eve had made time and time again.

"You mean she was *human*?" Miranda's mouth hung open in surprise. Her mind was running in so many directions, she thought her head would pop.

"Slow down, you're making my head spin. Forget I said anything."

"Forget you said anything? *Forget you said anything*?" Miranda was incredulous.

"Yeah, like it never happened." Elise released her hand from Miranda's, momentarily

[61]

forgetting that she needed to touch her in order for Miranda to breathe.

Choking on saltwater, Miranda lunged for Elise. "Don't *ever* do that again!"

"Oops, sorry." Elise shrugged as she guided Miranda back toward the boys.

"Wait! Tell me about Justine. What happened?" Miranda had to know all of the details.

"Later, I promise. Right now we have to get back to the boys or they'll suspect that we're up to no good."

Chapter Eight

Deep inside their cave, the girls were talking in whispers. Miranda had pestered Elise for days now, and finally she was going to get some answers.

The four had become inseparable, the two couples out for hours each day, just exploring and enjoying each other's company. It had been like torture hanging out with Evan and not knowing what was going on.

"I don't want Mom to know that we're talking about this." Elise insisted upon speaking in hushed tones.

"But can't she read your mind anyway?" Miranda asked.

"No, and I can't read hers, either," Elise explained. "And if she's not tuned into you, she won't pick up on anything. However, if she focuses on you, she'll know everything."

"This is all too confusing for me. How do you know when she's focused on someone?"

Elise sighed. "You *don't* know. It's a chance I'll have to take. Okay, so Justine was here, in our place with me and Mom, just like you."

Miranda had so many questions, but kept quiet until Elise was finished.

"Justine was happy here at first. She had family problems, so this was a great diversion, an escape from all of her stress, you know? We were best friends—close, like sisters. Like you and me."

A part of Miranda felt jealous. It seemed that she was just filling Justine's shoes.

[63]

"She left about a year ago and Mom hasn't been dealing with it very well. I think that's why she sought you out. To help her forget about Justine." Elise glanced at Miranda before putting her head down.

"So I'm just a replacement? Is that what you're saying? To your mom, to Evan, to you?" She had thought that these people, these creatures really cared about her.

"No, don't ever say that. Don't even think that. I feel your pain. You're special to all of us—just as special as Justine was, but even more so to me. And yes, even more so to Evan. You're all that's on his mind."

There were some perks to this mind-reading business. "Really?"

Elise gazed at her friend, nodding. "Yes, I mean it."

Miranda released the breath she had been holding. This wasn't the best news, but at least she wasn't merely a replacement to Elise and Evan. The bond between Miranda and Elise had just grown stronger, if anything.

"It hurt Evan that she left. He hasn't even thought about another girl—until you came along, that is. Now you're all he sees."

Miranda believed her friend. This was all so new and confusing, her raw emotions about her relationship with Evan. She was so young, and he was, too. Weren't they too young to be feeling this way about each other?

"My mother, on the other hand, is going to be the toughest challenge you will have to face here." Elise's tone dropped to a softer whisper.

"What do you mean? She doesn't care about me? She wants Justine back?"

"No, she cares about you, all right. Justine isn't coming back. Even if she wanted to, she never could, and all connection between her and my mom has been broken. That's how it works."

"See, that's just it. *How* does it work? How did I get here? When can I leave?" Miranda didn't mention that she was wondering whether she would even want to leave this paradise she had found with her new family.

"I've already said too much. I can't say anything else except that Mom is the one who gets to decide—well, more like you and her together."

Feeling her necklace, Miranda rubbed the jewel. There was so much to love here, so very much, but it wasn't her real home. More than anything, she prayed that her mother was okay, that she somehow was oblivious to all of this, just like Abby had said. Her mother's face, her voice, her laughter had been on Miranda's mind more and more.

"Your mother is fine. She doesn't have a clue, so you can stop worrying about that," Elise repeated for the hundredth time.

"So you say. I have a very hard time believing that, but what can I do?" Miranda shook her head and swam from one side of the cave to the next, trying to gather her thoughts.

It was so unsettling to have her friend read her mind constantly. Why did she even exert the effort of speaking if her friend was just going to continuously repeat her thoughts? Irritation, not unlike that she had been feeling toward Eve, bubbled in her blood.

"Can you do me a favor, please?" Miranda demanded.

"Sure. I'll act as if I don't know what you're thinking. Got it," Elise smirked.

"Ugh!" Miranda tossed a shell through the water, only to see it float gracefully over to where Elise snatched it up, mischief in her eyes.

* * *

"Can you help me in the kitchen, Miranda, sweetie?" Abby's soft call interrupted her thoughts of her mom and David. She had been wondering what they were doing, if they missed her somehow. Miranda knew that she was being summoned because Abby had picked up on her feelings of homesickness.

"Hey, Abby." Looking at the woman, she felt sad for her. It must have been difficult for her to lose Justine.

"Don't feel sorry for me. I won't permit it. Justine is gone, but it was her choice—and no, I didn't stop her, though I could have." Abby swam up beside Miranda and twirled her sweeping blonde hair through her fingers. It felt kind of nice, reminding her of when Mom would play with her hair as a young child.

"You miss her, don't you?"

"Yes, Abby, I do."

"It will get better with time, I can assure you that," Abby offered, continuing to play with Miranda's long blonde strands.

"No, Abby, it won't. I'm human, I don't know about you guys, but *I* don't forget." The words were out before Miranda could stop them. Knowing that she had crossed a line, she instantly regretted it. "I'm sorry. I didn't mean—"

[66]

Abby dismissed her with a wave of her hand. "Believe it or not, we feel just as deeply as humans, Miranda."

"I know, it was wrong of me to suggest—"

"It's okay. You're confused, you're being pulled in all directions. I can feel it." Abby sighed, swimming over to the other side of the room.

"How long did she stay?" She was referring to Justine. She needed a time frame.

"Just over a year."

"A *year*?" Miranda shouted, jumping to her feet. "You kept her here for a *year*? Against her will?"

"No, it took her that long to decide. I swore that I would never allow that to happen again. A year was too long. We all got so attached to her…" A lone tear slid down Abby's anguished face, making her appear much older than her years.

Miranda knew that Abby understood the unspoken question. "I'm giving you another month."

"Another *month*? But it's already been weeks!" Miranda shouted, knowing that she was acting juvenile.

"It's essential that you're sure. Thirty human days from now, you'll decide and I won't try to sway you either way. I promise. You have to want to stay here. If you don't, as sad as it will be to see you go, I won't stop you."

Didn't she see? What made her happiness more important than her own mother's? "But my mom, my dad, my family!"

"It would be as if you never existed. None of them will feel any pain." *As if I never existed? As if I never existed?* A prickling chill raced up Miranda's spine. *What was this place?*

[67]

"How could you? How could you do this? You know I want to go home, but you also know that I think of Elise as a sister and you know I'm falling for Evan! This is wicked!" Storming off, Miranda swam as fast as she could, past the stares of the creatures in town, past Elise and Thomas and finally past Evan. Stopping at the exit of the town, Miranda pushed on, knowing she was headed for destruction, but powerless to stop it.

"Get back here, Miranda!" It was Evan, catching up in leaps and bounds.

"No, leave me alone! All of you, leave me alone!" She was reminded of a time not that long ago when she had wished the very same thing from her family back home.

Plunging through the vortex once again, she gasped and water filled her lungs instantly, the pain intense.

"I got you, sweetheart. I got you." She was safely in Evan's embrace, breathing deeply.

"Don't let me go." Miranda sobbed heavily.

"I'll never let you go." He pressed his head over hers, holding her in a tight embrace.

Chapter Nine

They lay on the rocks, not talking. There was no need for words. Miranda was trapped in this place for another month. She couldn't fight what fate had thrown in her path. Her mind and heart were twisted. Why couldn't she go back home and take Evan and Elise with her? It wasn't fair, this set of rules that Abby had placed upon her. Who was Abby to demand such things? She didn't want to leave her new friends here, but it hurt so badly to imagine that everyone at home would just forget that she ever existed.

She couldn't bear that—but on the other hand, she couldn't bear leaving Evan and Elise behind. As much as it might hurt Abby to hear it, she wouldn't be the one that Miranda would long for. Abby had saved her life as a child and then saved it again, but she had also drawn her here, caused all of this, kept her like a prisoner.

A prisoner in paradise. But still a prisoner.

Gazing into Evan's smoldering gray eyes, she had to admit that her cellmate was sure easy on the eyes.

"Penny for your thoughts." Evan tore her away from her thoughts momentarily.

"I was just thinking, that's all." Miranda sighed and snuggled closer to Evan, feeling his warmth.

"How much time do you have?" Evan wondered aloud.

"Another month."

"A *month?*" Taken aback, he accidentally released her but then quickly grabbed her before her lungs filled with water. "But Justine had a year." His voice faded.

"Abby said it was too long, that everyone got attached."

Evan's eyes were distant. He remained silent, scanning the ocean around them.

"Evan, talk to me." She could feel his hurt.

"Let's head back." He lifted her to his side and they swam back in silence. Somehow the passing fish didn't seem as bright or colorful now.

Passing back through the vortex with a gush of water in their wake, Miranda let go of Evan's hand. She didn't want him to feel obligated to hold it anymore. Here she was fine on her own. He paused before turning to face her.

"Miranda?"

"Yes?" she gulped.

"For what it's worth, Justine has nothing on you." With a swoosh, he swam off leaving her behind with her thoughts.

* * *

As if she wasn't in a bad enough mood, when she arrived home she found Abby in the kitchen.

"Hi, sweetheart," Abby called out, basking in the role of the happy mother. *Of course she's happy, she gets to call all the shots.*

"I said hello, cat got your tongue?" Abby giggled.

"If you don't mind, I'd rather have some privacy. I'm not in the best of moods," Miranda grumbled, swimming past the table.

"Please, don't go." Perhaps it was the tone of her voice that stopped Miranda or maybe it was just curiosity, but she stopped and took a seat at the table. Abby swam up beside her, rubbing her hands together, chuckling softly.

"If this is going to be another talk where everything is made up of riddles, I'll leave now." Miranda's patience had thinned.

"It won't be. Listen, I've been thinking. You and I seem to have gotten off on the wrong foot. Something went wrong after I brought you back here. You've grown distant," Abby began.

"*Before* we got here? Are you forgetting when you tried to drown me on the way here? Or wait—perhaps it's the fact that you've kept me prisoner? Hmm, now, why wouldn't you and I be closer?" Placing her hand on her chin, Miranda pretended to think long and hard, coiling up for an argument.

"You're right," Abby said calmly. No giggling this time, just a simple statement.

"And what about when you—wait, did you just say that I'm *right*?" Miranda's jaw dropped to the floor.

Abby became uncharacteristically serious. "I've watched you. I've heard your thoughts. I've seen the anger, the sadness. You don't have to stay the month. You can leave now."

Miranda opened her mouth to speak, but words didn't come.

"That is, if you want to," Abby offered, creasing her brows.

"I, uh…" Miranda was at a loss for words. "I can't right now. I mean, I have Elise, Evan to think about."

"I know." Abby reached for Miranda's hand and squeezed it softly. "It seems you have a lot to think about."

"I do." She wanted to go home, but she also wanted more time. "My family doesn't know that I'm gone?" she asked again, just to be sure.

"Nope." Abby smacked her lips together.

"Then I'll take more time. I have things to tie up here, things to do." Miranda felt as if a weight was lifted. It was one thing to be trapped in this underwater paradise against her wishes, but it was another thing to be here now of her own free will.

"Oh, Miranda?" Abby met her gaze directly.

"Yeah?"

"The rules still apply. You can leave anytime you want, but you can't stay past a month if you do decide to leave." Abby's expression was filled with pain.

"But Justine had a year! I mean, if I'm having a good time, why do I *have* to leave in a month?" Her chest pounded.

"Because none of us could bear getting that attached to you. Take it or leave it."

Miranda squeezed Abby's hand. "I'll take it." She decided that she would open her heart and mind to Abby as well. The woman wasn't all that bad. She had her best interests at heart, even if she did go about things in a screwy, backward way.

"Good. Now how about some cookies?" Abby brightened.

"Sounds delicious." Miranda rose to her feet, intent on helping Abby prepare the snack.

"Sit. I like taking care of you." Abby leaned over to kiss the top of Miranda's head and giggled ever so softly.

* * *

"What happened between you and Mom?" Elise wondered as the girls explored outside of town, this time without the boys. It appeared that Evan didn't want to join them today and Miranda really couldn't blame him. She was torn between not wanting to get attached to him and wanting to spend every moment of her limited time here with him. It *was* limited time, she figured. How could it not be? Her mind wandered to Evan's handsome boyish face and his gray eyes.

"Snap out of it, we'll talk about him later. I'm asking about Mom right now," Elise demanded.

"I thought you weren't going to do that anymore." Miranda glared at her friend, who was behaving exactly as Eve would in this situation.

"Old habits die hard, I guess. I noticed that you and Mom seemed to have called a truce. What gives?"

"Oh, I don't know. She's not so bad. When I first saw your mom I was in awe of her. She's so beautiful, kind. She's kind of funny at times, but also she gets on my nerves."

"Aren't all mothers like that?" Elise scrunched her brows, holding onto Miranda with one hand and fiddling with a piece of seaweed with the other.

"I just became so angry with her, though. So frustrated at being kept here…"

"I guess I can understand that. I mean, she's my mother and sometimes even *I* want to have nothing to do with her. Again, that's moms for you." Elise chuckled.

"You said it." Miranda grew sullen for a moment as she thought of her own Mom. "It's funny. I miss her a lot, though."

Elise knew that she was speaking of her own mother, so far away. "What are you going to do?"

"I don't know. What would you do if you were me?" Miranda held onto her friend, who was quickly becoming the sister she never had. She knew that she would have held on to Elise's hand even if she could breathe on her own.

"It's a tough one. Think of all the pros and cons. That's what I do whenever I have a big decision to make. It usually helps."

Sighing deeply, Miranda mentally calculated. Knowing that her friend could read every single thought she had, she still spoke aloud. "Okay, pros: I love being here in this unbelievable place, in this magical town. The people—er, mermaids and mermen—are so peaceful and kind. Then there's you, you're becoming like a sister to me, and your mom, of course. Yes, I suppose she's growing on me."

Miranda took a breath and continued.

"Then, of course, there's Evan, my first true love." Staring at the coral in the distance, Miranda paused.

Elise snapped her fingers sharply. "That's quite a list. Continue."

"Okay, the cons: I miss my mom, David, Eve, my dad…" Once again, Miranda paused, a faraway look in her eyes.

"Would you be in the wedding?" Elise squinted at Miranda.

"Please. Stop. Reading. My. Mind!" This was infuriating.

"Sorry, sorry. Tell me about your dad and his fiancée."

Miranda spilled her heart out. She told Elise everything, from when her parents first divorced right up until the phone call on her birthday asking if she wanted to be in the wedding.

Elise let a moment go by before speaking. "It's a tough break, but from where I sit, it doesn't seem so bad. "

Spinning through the water, Miranda tightened her grip on Elise. "It doesn't seem so bad? Are you *kidding*?"

A thought popped into Miranda's head suddenly, one she was amazed she'd never had before: Elise's father was never around. She had been so wrapped up in her own problems she hadn't even noticed.

"My dad left." Elise stared at a long purple and red fish darting by.

"Did your parents get a divorce?"

"Nope. He went back." Looking away, Elise almost pulled her hand off of Miranda, but quickly returned it.

"He was *human*?" This was a shocking discovery.

"Yes, he was human. I never even knew him."

"Wow, it's no wonder your mother has so many issues when it comes to humans." A pang of sympathy went out to Abby, knowing how difficult that must have been for her.

"Yeah, I guess." It wasn't often that Elise was silent, and it made Miranda uneasy.

"Do you think I should be in my dad's wedding. Would you do it?" Miranda asked carefully.

"I'd be proud to be in my father's wedding. You'd be a fool not to. Besides, what has Sarah ever done to you?" Elise's mouth was still turned down in a frown.

"I...I...I don't know." Miranda couldn't think of one thing, besides looking at her phone that night at the restaurant. It kind of stunk that her own mother had never been on the receiving end of her dad's true affection—but personally, Sarah didn't do a thing wrong, except for the fact that she wanted to marry her dad. "My dad made his choice." The raw emotion was still right on the surface, making her blood boil.

"You'll be sorry. You should do it."

"I'm not even sure I'll be around to choose."

It should have made Elise smile, but instead she frowned, thoughtful.

Chapter Ten

It had been four days since she had seen Evan. Where was he and how long did he plan on ignoring her? This town was too tiny not to be seen for days. They could have precious little time left and he was being stubborn.

After some long and hard thinking, Miranda had decided that she'd rather spend the next several weeks *with* Evan than *without* him. Gathering up her courage, Miranda swept past Abby in the kitchen, who was drumming her hands on the countertop, deep in thought.

"Where are you headed?" Abby glanced up at the sudden movement.

"Just out." Miranda answered casually.

"Out? Why so vague?' Abby raised a brow.

"Why do you bother to ask when you already know?" Miranda sighed deliberately. When she got home, she would be forever grateful that her own mother didn't have the unique ability to read minds.

"He's confused, you know. That's why he went away," Abby offered.

"Where is he, Abby? I need to know. I have to go to him." She was desperate to see him, to speak with him.

Shaking her head firmly, Abby swam up beside Miranda. "I would give him this time, this space."

"But is this how we should be spending our last few weeks together? Not speaking?" Miranda threw up her hands in frustration.

"Are you quite sure that these will really be the last weeks, Miranda?" Abby spoke softly, no hidden riddles in this question.

Sitting down at the small table, Miranda placed her head in her hands and wept. At her side in an instant, Abby soothed her, placing small kisses on the top of her head.

"Abby?" Miranda peered into the mermaid's eyes. "What am I going to do?" Perhaps this wise creature could give her some insight.

A strange gaze washed over Abby's face. Tears welled up and she cleared her throat. "Honey, you know that I would like more than anything to have you stay, but your heart has to be in the right place. You have to want to stay here more than anything in the world. There can't be any doubt."

Miranda mulled that over. Sure, this place lacked all of the stresses of home, but if she was honest, there were some unique stressors here in paradise as well. Learning that life was never simple was one lesson that Miranda was sure she would come away with. But, there were bound to be other lessons learned, too. Only time would tell.

"There's going to be doubt, no matter what my decision is," she said at last. "As much as we like to argue, you've become a mother to me, as Elise has become my sister."

Abby squirmed, releasing her hold on Miranda. She glided over to the sink, turning away. It wasn't like Abby to be so silent. Miranda moved closer and touched Abby's face, only to be met with more tears.

"What's the matter?"

"I...I just got to thinking how much I'm going to miss you," Abby managed, fighting through her cascading tears.

Miranda held her. It was her turn to nurture now. "Abby, no matter what I decide, I'll think of you all the time. Maybe we can see each other again."

Even as she spoke, Elise's words came back to haunt her. *"Even if she wanted to, she never could. All connection between her and my mom has been broken. That's how it works."*

"You know better than that." Abby gazed at her, pain in her eyes.

"I suppose I do." Miranda muttered, holding on tightly to her mother figure, her friend.

"Go ahead, now, before I start to cry harder. Go find Evan, I know you will anyway." Rising and scooting away, Abby headed to the sink to clean some dishes. "He's at the edge of town, opposite the exit, in a tiny, hidden cave. That's his hiding spot. Always has been."

"Abby?" Miranda ventured.

"Yes, dear?"

"For what it's worth, you're okay by me."

Abby's eyes lit up, as if those words were exactly what she needed to hear. "I guess you're pretty okay yourself," she returned, smiling.

"I won't be gone long."

"Take your time. Go have fun."

Miranda doubted that her mother would ever have said those words. Yes, Abby was turning out to be a pretty cool mom.

* * *

Where was this cave? She was on the edge of town, opposite the exit, just as Abby had instructed, but there was no cave in sight. Peering through layers of sea plants, she batted a pesky vivid blue fish away. It proceeded to dart right back in front of her face.

"Shoo! Get!" she mumbled through bubbles. "Evan! Evan! Where are you?" *Why didn't Abby tell me that the cave was hidden?*

She spent a few more minutes searching and then decided to take a rest on a large boulder overgrown with sea moss.

"I should have guessed that you'd come looking for me." She sensed him next to her before he spoke.

"Evan!" Grabbing his face in her hands, she planted a wet kiss on his cheek. Evan responded with a kiss of his own, this one delivered firmly on her lips. Oh, how she had missed him. "Why did you go?"

"I think you know the answer to that question, Miranda." His tone had changed. It was more serious now. "What are you going to decide? Who are you going to choose?" He gazed into the distance.

"Oh, Evan, it's not about *who* I'm going to choose." How could she make him understand?

"Isn't it, though?" He looked her squarely in the eye. "It's *all* about who you choose."

"Evan, you can't possibly expect me to choose between my mom and dad and you, Elise and Abby!"

"But you will have to. It's inevitable." She supposed he was right. In a way, she wished that someone would just choose for her, take the decision off her hands.

An idea bubbled up in her mind. *Why hadn't I thought of it before?*

"Wait. Evan, listen. What if I *don't* decide? What if I don't do anything at the end of the month?

Then what? I get more time, right?" A burst of hope spread through her body. Just the thought of having more precious time here thrilled her.

"No decision is indecision," he mumbled, glancing at a passing fish.

"Huh? But then what would happen?"

"Abby would send you back. She needs you to be sure. It would be as if you had decided to go back," he explained.

"Oh." It was no use. Her mind was cluttered with indecision, as Evan had called it, and the cobwebs were only getting thicker.

"I also think that you need to have a conversation with Elise," he said quietly.

"I *have* spoken with Elise. Countless times," Miranda insisted.

Shaking his head, he stared at her. "Please, listen to me. Talk to her, get her to open up."

"Open up? About what? Now you're starting to talk in riddles, just like Abby." *What was it with these complicated creatures?*

Evan seemed to shake himself. "I have an idea." He pulled her close against him, resting his chin on top of her head. "How about you stop thinking about it? Just enjoy yourself, be free. On the day before the big decision, then decide."

It actually made sense. It was doing her no good to waste her time agonizing over the future. *Sometimes a break is what you need to figure things out.*

"You're right." Peering up at him, she settled deeper into his arms.

"Of course I'm right. Now kiss me." He leaned down, placing his soft lips upon hers.

Chapter Eleven

"*Come home, Miranda! We need you!*" *Reaching out for her daughter, Anne cried out. Miranda looked from her mother to Abby. Abby was trying to pull her in another direction. Elise's voice chimed out from the distance.*

"*Miranda, come on. We can explore every day! Forget about school, your wicked stepmother, and stay here with me. We'll be real sisters.*"

Where was Elise? Spinning around, she could hear her friend's voice, but she was nowhere to be found.

"*Where are you, Miranda? It's not the same at home without you.*" *Eve called for her now. Where was Eve? Breaking out in a cold sweat, Miranda spun around, searching the ocean depths for the origin of these voices.*

"*We're only just getting to know each other. Stay with me. We can be together forever.*" *Evan's face was before her, leaning in to kiss her. Abruptly, he pulled away.*

"*Miranda, come back.*" *It was the face of that football player on the beach who had just been walking over to speak with her that stormy night before the thunder. "They need you.*"

Who needed her? Her head was spinning as she caught her breath, doubled over from the intensity of her experience. All of these voices were shouting to her, calling to her simultaneously.

"*Stop it!*" *she cried, rocking back and forth, grasping her head. "Stop it!*"

"What is it, Miranda? What's happening to you?" Elise pulled her friend, snapping her back to reality.

Focusing, Miranda knew that something was very wrong. Was the realization brought on by a dream? No, that couldn't be—she never slept here. Was it a hallucination?

"Where is she?" Sweeping past Elise, Miranda rounded the corner. *"Where is she?"* she demanded, louder this time.

"She went to town. She'll be home any minute. What's the matter? For goodness's sake, it looks as if you've seen a ghost!" Elise scurried over, worry creasing her brow.

"I don't know what I've seen, but it doesn't even matter. I need to speak with Abby *now.*" Miranda stomped her foot down in the sand.

"Is somebody looking for me?" The sound of Abby's voice came through the entrance.

"You were *wrong.* How could I have believed you? You were lying to me this entire time!" Miranda choked on her words, gasping for breath.

"Honey, calm down. You need to calm down, What is this all about?" Abby asked, putting her bag down.

"You know exactly what I'm talking about! Another lie!" Miranda yelled, pointing at her. "You...you told me that my family didn't know, that they didn't miss me, that they didn't know I was even gone!"

"Well, they don't. Not really..." Abby's voice faded.

"Not really? *Not really?!"*

Elise fidgeted, glancing from her mother to Miranda.

"Just calm yourself and I'll explain. I didn't want to worry you needlessly."

"You didn't want to worry me needlessly?" Miranda repeated, her jaw slack. "Are you out of your mind?"

"Miranda, please, lower your voice. Sit down and we'll talk calmly." Abby approached, reaching out to her.

"Get away from me! Don't touch me! You'd better start talking or I swear, I'll leave this second!"

Flitting from one fin to the next, Abby spoke. "They have no idea how much time has gone by, but…" Abby was searching for words.

"Keep going." Miranda moved closer.

"Your family has a sense that you're in trouble. That's all they know. But 'trouble' actually isn't the correct word, now, is it? I suppose it isn't the time to get caught up in semantics, is it?"

"Stop it. Stop talking like that. You're driving me crazy. What does my family know?"

"I'm not sure exactly, but it's all okay. Please, trust me," Abby insisted.

"*Trust* you?" Miranda scoffed. "Get me out of here. I want to go back now. *Right now.*" Her mind was made up. Now she didn't have to worry anymore about which way to go. It was all so clear.

Elise gasped, scooting backward on her tail, heading out of the room. Without even glancing at her, Abby called out. "Get back here, Elise. This involves you too."

Elise winced as she slowly approached her mother. "Okay, I suppose it does."

"What are you doing? I said I wanted out of here! You told me that I could leave now, whenever I wanted!" Miranda's pulse sped up.

Elise glanced at her mother, who nodded. "You're going to leave Evan?" Elise asked. "Like this? Without even saying goodbye?"

That question gave Miranda brief pause. "Well, I guess I could say goodbye. But that's it, I'm leaving. My mind had been made up." Crossing her arms in front of her chest, Miranda dared either one to mess with her.

"Tell her, Mom. Please tell her." Elise pleaded, staring at her mother with urgency in her gaze.

"I guess now is as good a time as any." Abby fiddled with her fingers. "I think there's something else you should know."

Tapping her fingers on the countertop impatiently, Miranda waited for Abby to continue.

"I, uh…may have left out a crucial piece of information."

Elise scurried to her mother's side.

"Go on." Miranda was quickly losing patience.

"I think it would be a good idea if you sat down," Abby suggested, glancing down at her bright tail.

"Fine." Miranda plopped herself down at the table and waited. "Now talk."

"Okay, so now try to keep an open mind. If you do, you may just consider this to be great news." With a nervous smile, Abby turned to her daughter, who nodded in agreement.

"Is there anything that seems—I don't know, familiar to you about Elise?" Abby started.

Squinting, Miranda took the girl in. She did, indeed, look familiar—a combination of herself and Eve. Miranda was beginning to think that this may actually *be* an alternate universe. If this girl was supposed to represent Eve, maybe they were trying to tell her that somehow. Had Eve also been transported to this underwater oasis?

"Are you telling me that Elise is actually Eve?" she said at last.

"Not quite, honey. Elise is your sister—your *real* sister."

The last thing Miranda remembered was Elise's arm around Abby's shoulder. The two mermaids floated together, side by side in support of one another. Then the world faded to black.

* * *

"How long has she been out for?"

Was that Evan's voice? Bits and pieces of the conversation were coming back. Opening her eyes, she was met with three faces staring back at her.

"What…what's going on?" Trying to sit up straight, her head ached. Returning her head to the pillow, Miranda fought to remember everything. Abby and Elise had been trying to tell her something important. *Elise was Eve?* No, that wasn't right.

Elise is my sister.

That had been what Abby and Elise had been trying to tell her. Yes, Elise had been *like* a sister—but that's not what Abby had said. Abby had specifically told her that Elise was her real sister. Her *real* sister! But how could that be? The heart-shaped birthmark came to mind.

"I think she's going to be fine. Let's just let her rest a bit." Elise's voice this time.

"Don't leave." Miranda's voice came out as a tiny squeak. Sitting up again, she cleared her throat. "Nobody is going anywhere until I get some answers. It looks as if everybody but me knew what was going on around here."

The three creatures shrugged, turning to one another.

"Figures. Somebody had better start talking," Miranda grumbled.

Evan chuckled softly. "Well, I guess we know where she gets that bossiness from."

He poked Elise, who jabbed him back promptly. "Very funny, Evan." She crossed her arms.

"Abby, you start. You're the mother around here," Miranda snapped.

"Please just try to have an open mind." Abby's eyes pleaded with her.

"You already said that. Go on," Miranda insisted, her irritation growing by the second.

"Okay. Just hear me out, let me tell the story, and then I'll answer anything else you need to know. I met your father many, many years ago."

"My *father?*" Miranda cried, incredulous.

"You have to let me finish." Abby reminded her.

"Fine, go ahead."

"Your father almost drowned, right on the very beach that I saved you."

Something in Miranda's head turned on. "I...I remember my mom telling me that story. She always told me to be careful." Miranda shook her head in disbelief. "I'm sorry, go on."

Clearing her throat, Abby visibly relaxed a bit. "He came back with me, just like you did. At first, I just rescued him—but he looked into my eyes, and *bam*! I've never felt like that before. He said he felt the same…"

"Oh, that's wonderful to hear, That was just after my parents had gotten *married*." Miranda glared at Abby.

"Miranda, you need to let her finish, please. I have a feeling that this will answer a lot of questions about your life, not just down here." Evan rubbed her shoulder.

"I think I know all that I need to know," she barked. "Some mermaid came along and swept my father off his feet, put him in a trance and made it so that he would never have feelings for any other woman again, including my mother."

Abby had some nerve, trying to play this off like everything could just be explained away. Miranda decided she'd heard enough, lifting a leg off the bed and onto the floor.

"Sit!" the three creatures shouted at once. Miranda returned meekly to bed.

"We never meant it to happen. It just did," Abby went on. "Where I come from, each person is destined to one true love. That's it. Consider it a blessing, consider it a curse. I think it's a bit of both. Your father was that to me and I suppose I was that to him. It wasn't his fault that he couldn't love your mother the way he should have loved his wife. It was destined."

That last piece of information was tough to swallow. "But why did he ever leave, if he was that in love with you? I mean, I wasn't born yet. He could have stayed. It would have been kinder to my mother."

Elise and Abby exchanged a look. "He had just found out that he was going to be a father. To you. Your mother had just informed him that she was pregnant. For what it's worth, it seemed they had a happy marriage until I came along." Abby winced. "That didn't come out the way I had intended. It was happy, but not true love."

"You didn't tell him that you were also pregnant?" Knowing Abby the way she did, Miranda had a hard time imagining her keeping quiet.

"I didn't know until after he was gone," Abby said quietly, her eyes misting over.

"Then why didn't Dad ever say anything? And is that why you found *me?* Did you save me when I was small only to have a connection to Dad? Did you drag me here again on my birthday?" She was spouting questions faster than Abby could answer.

Evan grabbed her hand, squeezing it tightly. "Go easy on her, hear her out."

"Miranda, honey, it wasn't like that. I couldn't see him anymore,. The mental tie had been broken the moment he left here—but you, I could see. I had to have some kind of connection with him. I loved him. I suppose I always will." Abby hung her head.

"Why didn't he ever say anything? Why?" Miranda pressed Abby, not letting up.

"He doesn't remember. You won't, either."

Sadness touched Miranda and she allowed Abby to stroke her hair.

"Oh." Dad didn't even know why he couldn't love Mom. *How sad for them both,* Miranda mused. *But wait, wouldn't that mean that Dad couldn't possibly be in love with Sarah?*

Reading her mind, Abby spoke up. "Not true love. Think of it more as companionship."

Miranda actually felt bad for Sarah, for Dad. *What kind of life would this be for them?*

"Don't worry, they'll be fine. Most people go an entire lifetime and never find the one they're destined to be with. They'll be happy." Evan cleared his throat, turning his head to avoid eye contact with Miranda.

"But, if that's true, then..." Staring at Evan, Miranda felt raw panic rise. "Evan?"

Evan swam away, to the far corner of the room.

Gazing into Abby's eyes, Miranda grabbed her hands with both of her own.

"Are we?" Miranda demanded.

"Yes, you two are destined. You're meant to be," Abby answered, averting her gaze to the sandy bottom.

"Oh my..." Miranda cried. No wonder it had felt so special to be near him. She had thought it was just first love—but it was actually *true* love. Evan spun to gaze at Miranda. Moving closer, he met her and buried his head in her hair.

"What am I going to do? I have a sister, a real sister, and my one true love. Abby, tell me what to do!" This was all too much to take in. Her head was spinning.

"Take a deep breath, relax." Evan said calmly with pain etched in his eyes. "Could we be alone for a moment?" he asked, glancing at Abby and Elise.

The mermaids left the room, heads down. Only when they were completely out of sight did Evan lean down, close to Miranda's face. He was so close that Miranda felt her heart stop.

"This is why I didn't want to tell you. You have to go where you're happy."

"But how can I ever be happy now without you? You heard what Abby said—it's a blessing, but it's a curse. I'll never fall in love again, not really, and neither will you."

Evan's gray eyes touched her very soul. "Your family needs you. Go now, before it's too painful."

Clutching Evan's hands for dear life, Miranda knew that she would stay the remaining few weeks. How could she not? Then—well, then she would have to come to terms with saying her goodbyes. For now, all she needed was right here in front of her.

Miranda's smile must have clued him in. "You're a fool." Evan gritted his teeth and leaned in for a kiss.

Chapter Twelve

"Promise me you won't tell Abby." Evan demanded.

Now here they were, above the surface of the water. Miranda had begged and begged Evan to take this trip, and he had turned her down countless times before she had worn him down. Miranda would never tell Abby, but she did worry that the mermaid would read her mind. How could anyone keep a secret from a mermaid?

"What's the big deal, anyway?" Miranda clutched Evan's hand, their heads bobbing in the moonlit waves.

"It's a secret, that's why."

"It seems like you're enjoying yourself just as much as I am, you know." Smiling at him through the darkness, Miranda leaned in for a salty kiss.

"I *am* enjoying myself. I'm with you, aren't I?" He kissed her head.

Miranda sensed that Evan was still holding back. Part of the reason that she had wanted to be alone with him was to talk. Another part of her longed to see the earth again. What had once seemed ordinary and mundane now thrilled her senses just as the underwater world had first done. The earth in all of its beauty was not to be taken for granted—and neither were her friends and family, she was finding out.

Spotting the lights of a boat off in the distance, Miranda squealed, splashing in the water.

"Shh! Somebody will hear you." Evan clamped his hand over her mouth playfully. Miranda splashed him, and Evan retaliated. Miranda squirmed to get away, but remembered that she needed to remain in contact with Evan. It had almost slipped her mind.

"Why, you—!" she cried in mock indignation. Pinning her hands to her sides, Evan leaned in. Knowing that they were destined to be together only intensified the sweetness of the kiss.

"We should probably be getting back." Evan smoothed her hair, holding her close while she shivered slightly in the cool night air.

"I have a question for you." Miranda brushed his dark hair through her fingers.

"Sure." Evan reached for Miranda's shimmering necklace.

"Were you born here?" She kept sensing that something about him was different than the others—more introspective, perhaps.

"No, I wasn't." An emotion crossed his face but it was difficult to name. Miranda remained silent, giving him time to continue. "It was several years ago. I was playing in the surf, hanging out with my buddies when John started getting rough. You know how guys are, always cutting up. Even then I had little patience for it. My mom had always said that I was wise beyond my years. "

"I can see that. Were you troubled? I mean, I guess that was part of the reason that Abby decided to bring me here."

"I wouldn't say 'troubled'—just typical boy stuff. But with you—Abby sought you out. With me, it was different. Call it timing, call it wrong time, wrong place. John started teasing this girl, making fun of her bathing suit, I don't know, but I told him to knock it off and he mouthed off to me. One thing led to another and we fought."

"I still don't understand." Miranda was trying to picture the scene: young boys fighting in the ocean waves.

"John hit me, hard. My head struck a rock, I drifted and then I was drowning. Abby pulled me to safety and the rest is history, as they say."

"So why did you decide to stay? I mean, you don't seem angry or bitter about your family."

"I wasn't." His eyes drifted out to sea.

"But then why? Why would you stay?" Miranda had a hard time believing that this boy would just up and leave his family and friends.

"I didn't have a choice. Abby wasn't always as fair and kind as she is now. She was bitter about your dad for so long, she tried to get people into her life—to fill the void, I suppose, like with Justine. She had Elise, of course, but she wanted more. She always wanted more."

A chill ran through her spine, but somehow it didn't surprise her that Abby kept Evan against his will. Abigail was a complicated creature. She had her good points, yes, but she also had a darker side.

"Oh, you poor thing. Do you still think about them—your friends, family?" As soon as she asked the question, she knew that it wasn't necessary. Of course he did.

"Every single day, every single hour. I didn't speak with Abby for almost six whole months. She tried to win me over: baking for me, buying me things in town. She even tried setting me up with Elise at one point." He chuckled at that.

"Elise? I had no idea. She never said anything." Miranda wondered why.

"Her heart was already taken by Thomas. Besides, I was friends with her. I didn't harbor any feelings for her."

Miranda liked the mature way that he spoke. Evan *was* wise beyond his years. "I'm sorry for all of it."

"It's okay. Just think: I wouldn't have met you."

"Yes." But they both knew that her time here was ending.

"You should go. You have to get out of here," Evan insisted after a pause.

"But how can I leave you behind? Especially with the knowledge that I won't even remember you?" It was all so sad.

"Because you have no other choice." Kissing the tips of her fingers, he grabbed her and dove under the surface. She supposed he was right, but didn't want the thought to muddle the waters. This was a rare moment with Evan, and she wished to enjoy it.

"Do you see what I see?" Miranda pointed to a dolphin, swerving through the water. Evan kept one hand on her and whistled with the other. The young bottlenose bounded over, chirping and clicking.

"Hold on." Evan pulled them onto the dolphin and they headed back down, to the deep, dark water, to a village that was pure joy and heartache wrapped in one.

* * *

"Where did you two head off to?" Abby eyed the couple suspiciously. Miranda forced her mind off their recent encounter and on to other things so that the mermaid couldn't read her mind: Elise, Eve, school.

"We wandered off outside of town for a while, over to the field." Evan offered, grabbing a homemade pastry off the table and munching into it.

Abby scooted him away from the table. "Evan, it'll spoil your appetite. Those are for dessert. Will you be staying for supper tonight?"

Ordinarily he declined, but after glancing at Miranda, he smiled and accepted the offer.

"Go ahead and clean up. Supper will be served shortly. Now scoot, and tell Thomas that he's welcome to come, too." Humming to herself, Abby stirred the stew.

Evan leaned over to kiss Miranda goodbye and swam off in search of Thomas.

Miranda was consumed with her worries. Evan did have a point: there was really no other way. In a short while, she would return to Earth.

"Abby?" Miranda said.

"Hmm?" Abby looked up, a saccharine smile planted on her lips.

"I, uh..." Stammering, Miranda felt her cheeks flush.

"You know, you really shouldn't lie to me. You or Evan, for that matter." Abby's grin remained intact.

"Lie?" It was no use—she couldn't hide anything around this place. Boy, would she be glad to return to the human race. "It wasn't his fault. Please don't be mad at Evan. I asked him to take me up there."

"Don't make excuses for him. He should know better, and so should you. Do you have any idea what would happen if we were exposed? I mean, I certainly couldn't take the entire human

[96]

race down here and hold them captive, now could I? We would be ruined. They'd never leave us alone."

"It's not Evan's fault. Please don't punish him," Miranda pleaded, not liking how Abby was starting to smack pots down on the counter. She didn't trust Abby when she became angry.

"Punish him? *Punish* him? What do you take me for? Some kind of ogre?" Abby grabbed some plates from the cabinet and slammed them down on the table.

"No, I didn't mean that."

"And why should you care about Evan? I know exactly what you're planning, and it doesn't include Evan." Pausing for a moment, Abby stared at Miranda. Neither one spoke.

Finally the silence was too unbearable to endure.

"I'm going to find Elise." Miranda edged her way out of the kitchen.

"Go, go ahead, like the rest of them. Leave me, you don't care..." Miranda shuddered as Abby's rants echoed inside the cave. Where was Elise? She needed to talk to her sister this minute.

Gazing out at the town, she saw many young mermaids, but not Elise. Feeling dejected, Miranda knew that she was probably off with Thomas somewhere. Evan had gone in search of Thomas, so perhaps they would all be back soon.

"Hey, Miranda!" Thomas shouted as he and Evan swam alongside her. But Elise wasn't with them, which was odd.

"Hey guys, have you seen Elise?"

"No, I figured she was home," Thomas answered.

"Oh, maybe I missed her." Miranda doubted it, but what else could she do?

"Are you heading back home? We're coming with you," Evan said.

She had been planning on going back but something caused her to hesitate.

"You know what? I'll catch up. I just need a minute."

"Is everything okay? Do you need me to wait with you? Evan asked, concern etching his face.

"No, I'm fine, Just tell Abby that I'll be there shortly," Miranda said. "And you might want to be careful what you say to her. She's in a foul mood. She knows we went up to the surface and she knows…"

"She knows what?" Shoot, she hadn't wanted to say anything just yet, and not in front of Thomas. But from the look on Evan's face, it was apparent that he had already figured it out. His eyes clouded.

"You're doing the right thing." His tone had grown softer, fainter. Thomas excused himself without a word, swimming off to Abby's cave.

Her heart broke into pieces. "We still have some time," she whispered.

"Yes, I suppose we do." Evan's gaze dropped.

"Don't be sad. We'll both be sad enough when the day arrives. Please don't ruin what time we have left with sadness." It was easy enough to say, but another thing entirely to do. "Go ahead, tell Abby that I'll be right there, and remember be careful with her tonight. She doesn't seem right."

Chuckling at that, Evan shook his head. "Does she *ever* seem quite right?"

"I guess you have a point there."

Chapter Thirteen

Just as she was heading back, Miranda heard a voice behind her.

"Miranda, what are you doing here?" Elise asked.

"Where have you been? I've been looking all over for you!" Miranda exclaimed. "We need to talk."

Her eyes darting from side to side, Elise fidgeted in the sand. "It's suppertime. Mom doesn't like it when we're late for supper."

"Yeah, well, she doesn't like a lot of things tonight. She said that that I'm leaving her, just like everybody else." Miranda glanced down and then back at Elise.

"Well, are you?"

"Am I what?"

"Are you leaving?" Elise bit her lip, waiting for a response.

Miranda was torn. She had found a best friend who had also become her sister. But she also had a mother, a father, a brother, and a best friend at home.

"I think you should leave." Elise said before Miranda could speak.

"Elise, this is going to be the hardest thing that I will ever have to do. But I have to go back. There's no other way."

"I know. Tell her that you want to leave tonight. Do it immediately." Elise spun around, searching the water.

"Tonight? Immediately? No, Elise, no, I still have some time. Evan and I need this time together..." It was a desperate plea.

"Girls! Supper!" Abby's voice boomed across the ocean waves. Elise's face registered fear.

"Your mother is in some mood tonight." Miranda shook her head.

"You haven't seen anything yet." Elise mumbled so quietly that Miranda barely heard the words.

It wasn't like Elise to be so silent. *What's going on?*

The two girls swam into the house, heading directly for the kitchen when they saw Abby. The mermaid was seated at the table beside Evan and Thomas, busily munching on a roll. Miranda was expecting Abby to be fuming that she and Elsie were late, but instead she appeared calm, her eyes fixed on Evan.

Evan, however, seemed more anxious than Miranda had ever seen him. His eyes were on the ground, avoiding eye contact with Miranda.

"Hey," Elise greeted everyone cautiously.

Abby glanced at them. "The stew is in the pot. It's cold, but, hey, what does that matter, right? I just spent the last few hours preparing a delicious supper and *nobody* thought to be on time." Evan cleared his throat as Thomas fidgeted in his chair.

"We said we were sorry, Abby," Thomas offered. Miranda figured they were also tardy, but not nearly as late as she and Elise had been.

"Silence!" Abby bellowed. Evan dropped his fork as it floated down with a clang. The kitchen was silent as Miranda glanced from one face to the next.

"Mom, please." Elise's voice shook.

"Please? Don't 'please' me, young lady! It was rude to be late and not one of you even cares about my precious time." Abby rose from the table, hands on her hips. Miranda clenched her fists, pressing herself back against the counter.

Evan stood as Abby approached Miranda, who was backing up even further from the counter.

"I...I want to leave, right now. You promised. I want to go back." Her voice was a mere squeak as Abby grew closer. Daring a glance at Evan, Miranda was sorry that they couldn't have a proper goodbye. She was scared, though, and she wasn't a fool—the time to go was now. Evan nodded his head in silent agreement, keeping his focus on every move that Abby made.

"I want to leave, right now. You promised," Abby mocked, giggling that strange, cryptic laugh, the one that Miranda had first heard the night that she had arrived. It suddenly dawned on her that Abby was crazy. The sound of Elise whimpering did nothing to ease her fear.

"Abby, don't!" Evan was in the space between Miranda and Abby in a flash. With a swift cracking sound, Abby struck him aside.

"Mom! What are you doing?" Elise screamed as Thomas jumped up, ready to defend his friend. Abby ignored the pleas of her daughter as she closed the distance between herself and Miranda.

Thomas charged Abby, only to be thrown to the side, his body smashing into the wall. Miranda's heart was pounding. She had never been so scared in her life, but she also felt a surge of courage.

"Abby! You've been like a mother to me and you've been like a nightmare. You've been my friend and you've been my jailer. Do the right thing, I'm sorry about my dad, but if you ever cared for him in the least, let me go. For heaven's sake, let me go!" Miranda shouted.

Abby pounced on her, but Miranda was quicker, more agile, squirming from her grasp.

"Speaking of your father…" Abby began with a wicked cackle.

"No! Miranda, she's not going to let you go, ever—not unless your dad replaces you!" Elise shouted, covering her mouth as Abby glared at her. Miranda knew that later Elise would pay for her little outburst. For now her rage was focused on one thing only: Miranda.

"You can't do that! I won't allow it! I'll stay rather than have my dad come back to you, you evil witch!" Miranda screamed. As much as she and her dad had been through, it seemed as if all of the tension and strain had been washed away. She loved her father, so very much. She was sorry. She would be in the wedding. It sounded like the most wonderful thing in the world right now.

"Too late!" Abby screamed. Miranda knew she had been reading her mind, picking up on her thoughts of reconciling with her father. Grabbing a fistful of her long, flowing hair, Abby forced Miranda to walk with her. "You are the only connection I have to your father. He will come. He will stay in order to set you free."

"You…you've been using me all along. Never! I'll never allow it!" Miranda spat.

"Then you'll be my prisoner. Get to your room, you little brat!" Abby shoved Miranda down the hallway.

"Leave her alone!" Evan shouted, throwing his full weight against Abby, only to be brushed off again. As he fell to the ground, he hit his head on a rock and went limp.

"No!" Miranda raced to his side, kneeling down, sobbing at his silent form. "Look what you did to him, look what you did!"

* * *

"Daddy! I'm so sorry. I should have understood. I do want you to be happy," Miranda sobbed into her pillow.

"It won't do any good." Elise was by her side, rubbing her arm. "She'll summon him here using your thoughts. You'll have to make a choice."

"I told you already, I'll stay. There's no way I can let Abby take him," Miranda explained through her tears.

"Please think this through. You have your whole life ahead of you. Your dad—well, he's already lived so much of his."

Sitting up straight, Miranda shook her head to clear her thoughts. "Wait a minute, I get it. If I leave, then you'll have my father back—*your* father, all to yourself." A sick feeling washed over Miranda as her very worst fears came crashing in.

Elise grabbed hold of Miranda's shoulders, shaking her. "Don't you see? She's trying to turn us against each other! I would never do that. Besides, I would much rather have my sister, my best friend with me."

Something told Miranda to trust Elise, that she was speaking the truth. Nodding, Miranda gazed up at her sister. "I believe you. I...I need to get out of here. I wish you could come with me."

"It doesn't work that way. I was born a mermaid and I stay a mermaid, forever."

"I see." Placing her hand in Elise's, Miranda sat silently.

"What are we going to do?" Elise wondered.

"We have to come up with a plan. We need to fight her." It hit her that Abby was still Elise's mother. "I'm sorry."

"Yes, she's my mother, but what she's doing is wrong. She's out of control. She'll be better again after you leave—I feel it. This is too much for her to bear. Having you so close, it reminds her of our father constantly. I've seen her spiral downward since your arrival," Elise explained.

"But what can we do?" Miranda's mind whirled with possibilities, each one quickly dismissed.

"Nothing will work. She's too powerful, even for me. The only way is to have her come around, realize that she's wrong," Elise admitted.

"And what are the chances of that happening?" Miranda ventured.

"Probably zilch." Elise twirled her hair over and over again, sighing deeply.

"So there's nothing we can do."

Elise appeared thoughtful for a moment. A small smile sparked her face. "Well, there's one thing—the only thing that just might work."

"What? What's the only way? Tell me." Miranda wished once again that she, too, could read minds.

"Your dad. You have to summon him here. It's the only way."

Shaking her head briskly from side to side, Miranda was firm. "No way. That's not going to happen."

"Don't you see? It's the *only* way. He's the only one who can talk sense into her." Elise jumped to her tail, swimming back and forth across the bedroom.

"But that's what Abby's counting on. She's been using me to get to him," Miranda protested.

"True, but still, it's the only way. Do it. Reach out to your dad. He'll feel you. If nothing else, he'll come to the beach where you were and then Abby can handle the rest. She's counting on you to bring him just close enough and then…"

"She'll have him in her reach! No, Elise!" Miranda shouted.

"The two of you, keep your voices down! I'm trying to concentrate in here," Abby's voice came from outside their door. "And don't get any bright ideas. I won't soften toward your father. Once he's here, he'll be mine forever. Unless, that is, *you* would like to stay, dear Miranda." Abby's cackle drifted off.

"You see? She can hear everything we say, everything we think. It's a losing battle. Bring your dad here. Do it. You can still decide to stay, and then he'll be free," Elise pleaded.

"I don't trust her. I don't believe that she'll let either of us go." If she had learned anything about Abby, it was that she couldn't be trusted.

"There's only one way to find out."

Chapter Fourteen

"Daddy, please forgive me," Miranda whispered. Miranda had been through this over and over again in her head, convinced that this was the only possibility for making things right, Miranda prayed she was making the right decision. Was this the right choice? Miranda's choice was the only feasible move to making both her world and her father's world right again. Elise was by her side, also a prisoner in the bedroom.

Elise grasped her hand firmly. "Do it. Now. Think of happy moments. Keep the images happy."

In Miranda's mind, she conjured memories of her father playing with her as a young child. An image of Father's Day, his birthday, a day at the park—all of the pleasant memories.

Sarah came to mind, threatening to ruin the positive vibe.

"Get her out of there. Think happy," Elise coached, squeezing her hand.

Her mother and father together. A vacation at the very beach where Miranda had stood not long ago...*I'm sorry, Daddy, for everything.*

"Stop, that's good. It's enough," Elise declared. "Now, we wait. If everything goes according to plan, he should arrive soon."

"I feel sick." Miranda's head was in her hands, and she moaned.

Elise rubbed her back. "It's okay. You can do this. We can do it together," she soothed.

* * *

They didn't have to wait long. Within a few hours the girls could hear Abby singing happily to herself as she got ready for their father's arrival.

A sharp pounding on the door caused Miranda to jump. "It's almost showtime." A tray of food appeared beneath their door.

Abby had been feeding the girls and allowing them bathroom privileges for the past several days, but that had been the extent of their interaction with the outside world. More than once, Miranda's mind had wandered to Evan, hoping that he was okay. Elise had informed her sister that Evan was still unconscious, trapped in a bedroom close by with a frightened Thomas.

"Will he be okay?" Miranda had been filled with concern for Evan when Elise first told her. "When is he going to wake up?"

"I don't know. Thomas is scared. I can sense it. He's still so worried about Evan. I can't read Evan's mind, so I know he's not awake yet."

"How could she do this? I mean, she trapped Evan so many years ago, and now this?" For the life of her, Miranda hadn't been able to understand how Abby's behavior had deteriorated so quickly. "Your mother isn't *completely* evil, is she?"

"No, there's a part of her that's not, but right now it's been pushed so far down it's hard to reach. It's that part we have to tap into," Elise had explained.

Now, Abby's voice flitted past their door. "I'll be back. It seems I have some business to attend to." Eerie laughter filled the air and Miranda cringed, drawing herself in deeper.

Shaking her head, Elise took hold of Miranda's hand.

* * *

It seemed like an eternity before the girls heard any noise in the house. Then Miranda recognized the sound of her father's voice and sat up like a rocket.

"Miranda! Miranda! Where are you?"

"It's Dad!" Miranda yelped. Both girls stood at the door, ready for action. "Daddy! I'm in here. Be careful!"

The door sprang open and Miranda jumped into her father's embrace.

"Let the man breathe," Abby said from behind him, shaking her head.

"Are you okay, Daddy?" Miranda did a quick once-over.

"Yes—I don't understand what's going on here. Are you okay?" He smoothed Miranda's hair.

Suddenly he spotted Elise, who had been standing there, waiting.

"Who's this? You look so…familiar."

"Of course she looks familiar. She's your daughter, for Pete's sake," Abby cackled triumphantly.

Miranda's dad glanced from Elise to Miranda and back to Abby.

"I don't have another daughter. I have Miranda and David…" he stuttered.

"Typical, Dave. I'm not surprised you would forget Elise—the daughter that we had together."

Confusion etched his face. He was speechless, gazing at Elise.

"Daddy, I'm sorry. I'm sorry about Sarah, about us. I love you, and I want to be in your wedding," Miranda blurted out, afraid that she would never be able to tell her father how she felt.

Abby came to Miranda's side, placing her hand on her shoulder. "I don't think that your father's wedding is of any importance now, is it?"

Brushing the mermaid off in disgust, Miranda watched her father. She could tell by the way his brows arched, the curve of his face, that he was starting to remember the past.

"Abigail, my goodness. Abigail." His eyes wide, Miranda's father approached the mermaid.

"So it seems you remember me at last. Isn't that nice? I spend, what, fifteen years or so waiting for you, thinking about you…"

This wasn't right. It wasn't her father's fault that he didn't remember. "Don't do that! He had no memory of you, you said so yourself!" Miranda shouted.

"Nevertheless…" Abby's grimace frightened her, but she didn't allow herself to look away.

"Abigail, what happened to us? We…we loved each other. My God, we had a daughter—Elise." He reached for Elise, holding her at arm's length and then pulling her toward him in an embrace.

Satisfaction creased Abby's face as she fixed her gaze on Miranda. "Good, now we can go back to being the happy little family."

"No! Daddy, don't listen to her! She's evil!"

Abby swam up to Miranda and clamped her hand over her mouth.

"Don't listen to her. She's had a bit of a hard time fitting in around here, haven't you, dear?' Abby's glare dared Miranda to argue with her.

Miranda was about to open her mouth when Thomas's voice echoed down the hallway. *Evan!*

"I want Evan out here. Let him out!" Miranda shouted.

Her father, confused, peered down the hallway. "Who's Evan?"

"It won't do him any good if he's not awake. Don't waste your energy on him, my dear."

"What has become of you? Abigail, you're not the same. What's happened?" Miranda's father backed away from the mermaid, his mouth grim.

"Are you going to tell him, or should I?" Abby challenged Miranda, her hand on her hip.

"You can tell him all about your wicked little plan, Abby."

"So be it. Dave, it seems that you have a choice to make," Abby announced. "You stay or Miranda stays. Pick one."

"I don't understand. Neither of us are staying here," Miranda's dad said, surveying the underwater cave. "I loved you once, and we had something special. Why are you ruining this? Let us go. We don't belong here and you know it."

"That's where you're wrong. Make the choice. Say the word and it's done," Abby ordered. "If you don't make the choice, I'll make it for you, and your precious little daughter—scratch that, *daughters*—will be my prisoners forever."

Miranda's dad opened his mouth to speak. Miranda swam up beside him, covering his mouth with her hand.

"Don't say it, Dad. She's lying. She'll never let me go, even if you say it. I know it, Elise can read her mind. You *can* go, though. Please just go back!"

"I could never leave you here. It's the only way," her father said.

Elise came up beside him. "It feels funny to call you my father, but you are, so listen," she said. "Don't say anything either way. You have time. My mother has to give you time to decide."

Smoothing her hair away from her face, Miranda's father gazed at Elise.

"I'm sorry that I didn't get to know you, but now we'll have time," he said.

"Dad, she's right, take some time," said Miranda. "I've been here long enough. Another day or so isn't going to kill me, please." She pleaded with her eyes.

"What's the use? It isn't like I'm going to change my mind."

Miranda wanted to shout that with some extra time, perhaps he could soften the mermaid and make her see the light. Abby glared at her, reading her most private thoughts.

Miranda's dad remained silent for a moment. "Is it true, Abigail? Do I have some time?"

"Time? Yes, Dave, you have some time to decide. But I'm telling you that it won't do you any good."

Miranda breathed for what seemed like the first time in hours. Good—with time, there was hope that somehow, in some way, her dad could change Abby's mind. She pressed herself against her father, as if to protect him from this monster.

"Now, the two of you, back to your room." Abby led the way to the bedroom. Both girls knew they were helpless to stop her. Miranda spun to steal a last glance at her father, willing him to change this horrid course of events. Her dad's eyes were bleak as he gazed at the sandy ground.

Chapter Fifteen

"Can you feel him yet?" Miranda urged Elise to try to connect mentally with Evan.

"I don't feel anything yet. I'm sorry, Miranda." Elise studied the ground beneath her fins. "If he wakes, I'll know it."

A moment of silence passed between the two as Miranda grew restless. Her father had been here for at least three days now, and she was growing more and more impatient sitting helpless in this tiny room. "How is it going? Can you tell anything?"

"Like I said the last twenty times, all I'm picking up on is his fear. Your—excuse me, *our* dad is afraid. He's afraid for you, me, and himself. He's also afraid for my mom. It's weird, but I can sense that he still cares for her, and wants to make her whole again."

"Yeah, like that would ever happen," Miranda chuckled sarcastically before noting the look on Elise's face. "Sorry, I didn't mean—" she began.

Cutting her sister off, Elise rose and swam around the four corners of the room. "You meant exactly what you said, but who could blame you?"

"Elise?" Miranda spoke after some silence.

"Yes?"

"I'll never forget you. No matter what, I promise." Miranda felt her emotions rise.

"Me too. I certainly won't forget. I'll miss you every single day." Elise drew Miranda in for a hug.

The sound of the bedroom door opening caused the girls to jump.

"Sorry for interrupting a moment here, but you're both free to come out." Abby motioned for the girls to follow her out into the hallway. Miranda and Elise followed her to the kitchen where their father was sitting.

"Dad!" Miranda flew to his side as Elise hovered, looking uncertain.

"Come here, Elise." Miranda's father opened his arms for her to join them. "I've made a decision. Now before you say anything, hear me out."

Miranda jumped to her feet. "No, Dad! She got to you, didn't she?" She glanced at Abby, whose smug grin told her everything she needed to know.

"Honey, please listen. A long time ago, I was very happy here—extremely happy. Abigail and I had a life together—"

"*We* had a life together, too!" Miranda was going to lose her mind.

"Sit down and listen to your father." Abby commanded before smiling sweetly to Miranda's father.

"I love you, Miranda, more than my own life. I'll never forget you, I'm doing this for you. I'll be happy here. Abigail has already started feeling better."

"Listen, I can't go back without you." She felt tears falling to her cheeks.

"If I let you go, if I do this, not only will you be set free, but Evan will wake up. He'll be okay, Miranda."

"You're keeping him asleep? To use as a bartering chip?" Miranda glared at Abby, incredulous, her hands in fists.

"Yup, and he'll be free if you leave your father be and let him stay."

"*Free?* What exactly do you mean by 'free'? Because he certainly isn't free living down here with you!"

"He'll be free to go back to his own home here, and get on with his life. It's the best I can do."

"Let him go, Abby! Let him go back to his family, his friends on Earth!"

"Evan has friends and family right here. Take it or leave it." Abby shrugged as she grabbed her father's hand from across the table. If Miranda had been sickened by the sight of Sarah and her father, it was nothing compared to seeing him with Abby now.

"It's the only way," her father said. "You've got your whole life to live. I wouldn't have it any other way."

"How could you cause such pain, Abby? You say you love him. If you truly love him, let him go," Miranda wailed.

Abby remained silent, as if giving the statement some thought for a moment.

"Nothing changes," she said at last. "Make your choice. Stay here with us or go back home. Either way, your father stays."

Did she mean it? Would she actually let me go? Miranda glanced at Elise, who nodded.

"Can I have a moment with Miranda alone?" Miranda's father asked solemnly.

"Sure. And here you are saying how horrible I am all the time, Miranda," Abby drawled.

Once everybody had left the room, Miranda and her father faced each other. Her father was the first to speak.

"Honey, I'll miss you, but what other choice do we have?"

"Try to butter her up, make her understand," Miranda pleaded, wringing her hands.

"You and I both know that Abigail is not a very understanding creature."

"But there's got to be another way! Think, Dad, think!" Miranda held out the faint hope that if Abby had truly loved her father once, then perhaps she could find it somewhere in that complicated heart of hers to let him go.

"I have, and so have you. Go now, before she changes her mind," her father insisted softly.

Miranda clung to her father for dear life. "I wanted to apologize for my awful behavior. I'm sorry about Sarah. She seems so sweet right now to me."

"I bet," Miranda's father murmured, a small smile spreading across his face.

"Those last few months we could have been together—it's all wasted time now," she sobbed.

"It's okay. We're okay now, aren't we? Better than ever?" He winked as Miranda lifted her face to his, and used his fingers to smooth away her tears.

"Yeah, I guess we are." Miranda saw her father's eyes well up with his own tears, which she gently brushed away. "For what it's worth, I'd love to be in your wedding, Dad."

Kissing the top of her forehead, he pressed her closer. "Do me a favor, would you? Tell David and your mother I love them?"

"But, I won't have any memory. I won't remember this place. It's how Abby keeps the secret."

"I know, but perhaps you'll dream of this, and if you do, tell them I love them."

"Of course I will. How about Sarah?"

He glanced at Miranda, then looked down.

"It's okay, Dad. I'm okay with you guys. Really."

"Then go ahead and tell Sarah that I love her, too." Miranda gulped as she recalled Abby saying that he could only truly be in love with her.

Miranda wondered briefly, with a shock, if anyone would remember him when she returned. Abby had said that if she left, nobody would even remember her. It would be like she had never been born.

"Dad, there's something else. If you go, it will be like you were never born. What would happen to me? Would I even exist? David?" It was a horrible thought.

"No worries there. Abby lied about that part. She confessed that she wanted you to stay at first, so she figured that if you thought you wouldn't be missed, it would be easier on you."

"Oh. She has all the bases covered, doesn't she?" Abby was a manipulative creature, that was for sure.

"She's not all bad, I believe I can still find the good in her—perhaps turn her around after all," Miranda's dad said.

He's just trying to make me feel better. Aloud, she said, "If she does, if you can reach her, promise me that you'll come back to all of us—that is, if you want to."

"In a heartbeat. Don't worry, I'll work on her." But the sadness in his eyes gave him away. Abby was a very stubborn woman.

"Go, sweetheart. I'll wait here. It seems you have a lot of goodbyes to say and I don't want to make it any harder than it needs to be."

How could she leave him? As difficult as it was going to be to leave Elise and Evan, Miranda knew that this tearful goodbye would be the worst. Her father kissed each one of her hands, tore his hands from hers and backed away, swimming out the door to the cave.

"Daddy! Don't leave me!" Miranda fell to her hands and knees, helpless as she watched him leave. There was no way that she could have walked away from him, and she knew he was trying to make it easier on her by being the one to leave first.

How could Abby be so wicked? How could she? Miranda punched her hands into the sand until she grew weak and tired.

"Miranda?" a voice squeaked. Gazing up, Miranda saw Elise approaching. She supposed this was goodbye number two.

"What am I going to do without him, without you?" she cried.

Elise wrapped her arms around her sister, gently rocking her.

"Maybe I should just stay," she sobbed. But she knew she couldn't bear to lose her mother. *Why do I even have to choose? This is so cruel.*

"You know better than that. Besides, maybe your dad will soften my mom, you never know." Elise looked away. Miranda knew that even she didn't believe her own words.

"Take good care of him for me," Miranda whispered, though she knew she didn't even have to ask. Elise would grow to love her father just as Miranda had. "And one more thing—"

"I'll take good care of Evan, too," Elise finished Miranda's thought.

"I'll miss you, sis." Miranda breathed deeply, feeling another round of tears coming on.

"I'll miss you, too. You're the best sister I could have hoped for. I'll always treasure our times together." Touching Miranda's shimmering necklace, Elise smiled.

"Oh, I forgot that I was even wearing this thing," Miranda said, unclasping it. "Here, take it. I don't want any reminders of Abby—no offense."

"I picked that out for you. Please, keep it." Elise begged.

Gathering her thoughts, Miranda wished for a way to tell Elise how much she truly meant to her.

"I already know. I feel the same way." Elise read her mind one last time, her eyes wet with tears. "Now I'm sending one more person in before Abby. Yes, he's awake and he's going to be okay."

Turning to leave, Elise stood by the doorway for a brief moment, gazing at her sister before blowing a kiss.

This last part was going to be even more heartbreaking.

Chapter Sixteen

Coming slowly into the room was the love of her life. Evan appeared weak, with dark circles etched under his eyes. Miranda rushed to his side.

She never wanted the embrace to end, but Abby would be back shortly. She knew they had some things to say to one another.

"Are you okay? Evan, I was so worried about you." Smoothing his hair back from his face, Miranda knew that she would see this face in her dreams.

"Yes, I'm fine. A bit achy, but otherwise okay. Don't worry about me, how are *you* doing?" He gazed into her eyes. Leaning forward, he pressed a small kiss to her lips. "I've been wanting to do that since I woke up." A smile crinkled his eyes.

How can I find the strength to leave him?

"You're making the right decision—the only decision that makes sense. Your mother needs you, and you need her. You've got your life to live. " Her face was inches from his own. "Go, and know that you're doing the right thing."

The squeaking sound of the door opening interrupted their special moment.

"Abby, you said you'd give us some time together," Miranda begged, aware that her voice was rising.

"Just to prove that I do have a heart, your Evan here is going to walk you to the edge of town. You'll get to the vortex and let her go," Abby instructed him.

"I can't let her go at the vortex. It's at least a thousand feet up! She'll never make it up without help," Evan contradicted.

"She's a smart girl. Where there's a will, there's a way. She'll figure it out—or not."

Miranda was astounded. *Some heart this woman has.*

"Abby, please!" She had been though the vortex alone before, when she had tried to run away. The thought of going through that again with nobody to save her was horrifying. *Why even bother to go when my chances of survival are so slim?*

"And no, you can't stay. You've made up your mind. You have exactly fifteen minutes to go before you lose the ability to breathe, and that includes time outside of the vortex. I suggest you use your time wisely. See, I'm even giving you a head start! Not so heartless after all, am I?"

Miranda was so angry she could scream. Instead she grabbed Evan's hand, rushing to the doorway.

"Oh, Miranda? One more thing..."

"What, Abby?" Miranda clenched her teeth.

"I'm going to enjoy making your father's life miserable every single day to get back at him for leaving me. You will not have peace in your decision, rest assured..."

Miranda spun on her heels, seeing red.

"Let's go!" Evan shouted, pulling at Miranda with all of his strength. "She's just trying to get to you. She loves him, you know that. Don't listen to her. Her words are poison, trying to slow you down."

Evan was right, she was sure of it. *Keep your head in the game, Miranda.* Right now she needed to reach the vortex in record time.

After a breakneck swim across town, Evan finally placed Miranda on her feet at the mouth of the vortex.

"Go. Hurry, you'll need every single second."

"Don't make me leave without saying goodbye."

Taking both her hands in his, Evan kissed them. "I will love you until the day I die."

Tears streamed down her face, making her vision cloudy. "And I will love you, too."

"You won't even remember me." Evan barely managed to get the words out.

"You'll always be in my heart and soul. I can feel it. Nobody can take that from me." Wiping a tear from his eye, she leaned in and lost herself in the bittersweet kiss.

Seconds before he released her, he whispered something in her ear. Nodding, Miranda squeezed him one last time.

Holding her hand until the last possible moment, Evan released her into the turbulent vortex. His face would be the last thing she saw from the mystical underwater village.

Water whooshed around her, tossing and spinning her until she thought that she couldn't take it one second more. Abby wouldn't really let her die out here, would she?

With minutes of fresh air left, she swam with all her might, up, up, up, desperate to climb the depths of the ocean. It took a lifetime to see the light.

Gasping and coughing, her lungs filled with water.

"*Oh, no! Evan! Somebody please help me!*" Miranda's thoughts echoed inside of her head.

"*Help! Help!*" Recalling Evan's last words, the ones he had whispered in her ear, she spun around, searching.

Remember the ride we took last time.

There was nothing but the sea surrounding her, nothing but the fish. *What did that even mean?* Thinking fast, she replayed the evening in her mind. The ride—the ride on the dolphin, yes. *Is that what he meant?* But there was no dolphin to help her out.

Wait, what did Evan do that night when he saw the dolphin off in the distance? She placed her fingers in her mouth and produced the best whistle that she could form, given the underwater environment and the gasps for air.

The dolphin came out of nowhere. Was it the same one from that night? It didn't matter. This dolphin was here to help her, to save her. Swooping under her, the dolphin lifted Miranda swiftly onto its back. She clung to it while they sped up to the surface. The sea around her whirled.

Her mind spinning, sucking for breath, Miranda gave in to the obscurity.

* * *

She dreamt of darkness, sea creatures, and Evan. In her mind, it was Evan's face that she saw the most. He was shouting, urging her to wake up, to breathe.

She heard other voices in the distance, and could have sworn one belonged to her mother. Hmm, that was nice, she hadn't seen her mother since forever.

Eve's voice was now a part of this funny dream, crying, pleading. But still, it was Evan's voice that was the loudest, the strongest. He was leaning down to touch her, to kiss her. It all felt so real. A blinding light was shining down, hurting her eyes, making her head pound.

Chapter Seventeen

What was that light? Why did it hurt so badly? She cracked her eyes open, and water gushed out of her lungs. Gasping and choking, she opened her eyes wider.

"Evan!" She sat up straight, gasping for air.

"Miranda!" Her mother's arms were around her, squeezing, holding on tight. Eve was standing there, sobbing.

"What? Where's Evan?" Peering through the darkness, she scanned the dark beach for Evan. "Where is he?"

"She's in shock. Ethan went for help," Miranda heard her mother say.

"Ethan? Ethan? Where's *Evan*?" She tried to stand, but fell. She hadn't used her legs this way in so long, it was no wonder she was wobbly.

"Sit back down, Miranda. Help is on the way." Miranda took in the sight of her mother sitting beside her and pulled her close.

"Mom. You have no idea how much I've missed you!" Grabbing her mother, she squeezed her.

"Are you okay?" It was Eve's voice, shaky with concern.

"Eve, it's so good to hear your voice." Miranda took hold of her friend's face and kissed her firmly on her cheek. Chuckling nervously, Eve glanced from Miranda to her mother.

"Mom. Where's Evan? I saw him here, where did he go?"

"Honey, his name is Ethan, and he saved you. He was playing football on the beach when you went into the water. He's a lifeguard."

"But he kissed me, I saw him." Miranda was sure of it.

Her mother mumbled something to Eve.

"Mom, he kissed me!" Miranda's voice rose in agitation.

"Honey, you need to calm down. Ethan didn't kiss you, he gave you mouth-to-mouth resuscitation. You were out cold. He saved your life."

"What did he look like?" Miranda needed to know. In her mind, she saw him clearly. It was her Evan.

"Miranda, he was that guy, the one with the football," Eve offered. "Remember, *Spellbound*?"

Miranda squinted, trying to summon a memory of the guy playing football. It started coming back to her: Eve's dare, a few of the guys laughing, one telling his friends to knock it off. One of the last things that Miranda recalled before being dragged out to sea was seeing the boy approach her in the darkness. She never got a very clear image of his face, though.

"*What did he look like?*" Miranda repeated, louder this time.

"I don't know, dark hair, tall." Eve glanced at Miranda's mother.

"What color eyes?" Miranda demanded.

"Eyes? I don't know..." Eve spluttered.

"Hey, the ambulance should be here any minute." It was *his* voice. She couldn't forget the sound of it. The boy squatted down and peered into her eyes.

"Evan!" She felt faint. Those gray eyes—it *was* Evan. Evan from the underwater world. Evan, her one true love.

"Er, no. My name's Ethan." Glancing up at Miranda's mother, Ethan shrugged.

Miranda couldn't breathe. The last words she heard came from her mother.

"She's in shock. Where's the ambulance?"

* * *

Waking up, Miranda squinted in the bright light. Her mother's hand grabbed hers. The light was blinding and all she could think of was having a sip of water.

"I'm thirsty," she managed.

Her mother hurried to pour water from a pitcher. Placing a paper cup in front of her, her mother moved a stray hair out of place. "How do you feel, honey?"

Her dry, cracked lips sucked at the cup of water, her trembling hands causing the water to spill onto her chest.

"Oh dear." Her mother scurried out the door and quickly returned with a straw in hand. "Here, try this."

Miranda sucked at the straw, feeling cool water fill her belly.

"Anything else I can get for you?"

Miranda willed herself to remember details that were just out of reach. She recalled waking up on the beach and calling for somebody named Evan. But who was Evan and why had she become so upset?

"Mom, who was that guy who helped me?"

"Ethan? Ethan's a great young man. He's here in the waiting room, as a matter of fact."

"But why? I don't even know him." *Why would the boy from the beach come to the hospital to see me?*

"Well, for starters, he saved your life—and it also might have to do with the fact that Eve seems to have a crush on his blond friend." Sighing deeply, her mother continued. "You nearly drowned, Miranda. I don't want to get into this here, with your condition right now, but later I need to find out why you would walk straight into the ocean on a dark and stormy night."

"I...I don't know." Miranda vaguely recalled doing it, but for the life of her, she couldn't grasp the reason for her actions. "Where's Dad?"

"Funny thing, I called for him at his house and Sarah answered. It seems your father's gotten cold feet, he took off without explanation and isn't answering Sarah's calls, she's very worried about him."

"Hm. That's weird, I thought he really liked her," Miranda mused. It struck her as odd that she wasn't thrilled with the news. She hadn't made it a secret that she disliked the woman, but now she kind of felt sad in a way. Miranda felt her heart quicken, sensing that something wasn't right. This wasn't like her dad, he had cared about Sarah so much.

Just then, Eve barged in the room, giggling with the two young men from the beach. The trio silenced as soon as they spied Miranda's face. She figured that she must appear quite the sight by their reactions.

She knew she'd seen the boys playing ball on the beach before, but she couldn't shake the deja vu feeling that she'd known them before—perhaps from another time?

Miranda's mother excused herself to go to the cafeteria for a few minutes.

"Miranda. How are you feeling?" Eve asked once she'd gone, her brows furrowed in concern.

"I guess I'm okay." *Why would I just walk into the ocean at night?* Eve had recounted that Miranda had simply walked toward the choppy water, ignoring her friend's shouts to stay out of the water. Ethan had also reported trying to call her back, but the two teens said that Miranda appeared as if she were in a trance.

"We were so worried about you. All of us." Eve nodded toward the boys beside her. Miranda still felt she had known these boys before, quite well—but that was ridiculous, wasn't it?

"I'm so glad that you're okay." The boy named Ethan came forward. His handsome smile made her blush, his striking gray eyes penetrating her gaze.

"Thank you for saving my life." Ethan smiled and her gut twisted with emotion. There was no denying that this boy was attractive, but it was more than that. Ethan seemed to look through her.

Eve was whispering something in the other boy's ear. The blond boy also looked familiar, but there were no deeper feelings like there were with Ethan.

"Miranda, this is Theo," Eve said. Theo's freckly face peered down at her before he took her hand.

"You gave us quite the scare," he said and smiled.

"Eve? Could we have a minute alone?" Miranda asked. The boys nodded and ducked out of the room quietly.

"Eve, why did I walk into the ocean, when it was dark and stormy?" Miranda demanded once they had gone, gripping her friend's hand. "That doesn't make any sense. What were we doing before it happened? Tell me exactly what we were doing."

"I...I guess right before it happened we were playing *Spellbound*, remember?"

"*Spellbound*. Yes, I remember." Miranda recalled the dare, and then landing on the spot to summon a mystical creature. "What did I conjure up, do you remember?" She squinted at her friend. "Come on, think. It's very important."

"I don't know. You said something strange. I can't remember." Eve shook her head. "Then you stood up. Thunder clapped, lightning struck, and you were off, walking directly into the ocean."

Miranda thought hard, trying to remember. *What had I been saying before I walked into the ocean?* Somehow she sensed that it was key to the mystery of her near drowning.

"Eve, it's crucial that you remember. Tell me anything that you can about what I said."

Eve bowed her head in thought. "I can't remember anything, except—wait. You said something like 'If I need me'? No, wait, that's not it. 'If I need you, let it...'"

"*If I need you, let it be, if you need me, look to the sea,*" Miranda interjected suddenly.

The boys swung the door open at that moment. Ethan's gray eyes met hers and she suddenly remembered. Everything. A switch had been turned on and memories of the underwater world came flooding in. She'd been told that she would have no memory of her time spent under the sea—but that chant had worked magic before, hadn't it?

"Oh my..." Searching her brain, she recalled just how much Evan had meant to her. Now he was here, in the flesh. "Evan!" she exclaimed.

Eve stood, eyes darting between her friend and the boys. "Er, Miranda? We told you that his name is Ethan."

Ethan and Theo glanced at each other. "We should go," Ethan said, and the two dashed back into the hallway.

"Miranda, you're scaring Ethan. Why do you keep calling him Evan?" Eve took Miranda's hand and held on.

"Because his name *is* Evan. Get him back here. I need to speak with him," Miranda insisted, peering past Eve's shoulder at the doorway.

"Stop this. You've been through an ordeal, and you need to rest," Eve scolded.

The sound of her mother's footsteps caused Eve to let out a breath. "Good, your mom is here."

"How are you feeling, honey? I picked up a few snacks for you at the cafeteria." Miranda's mother approached with some bags of chips and pretzels.

"Mrs. James? Can I speak with you a moment out in the hallway?" Eve asked quietly.

"Oh, great, so now I'm crazy. Mom, anything she has to say to you can be said right here, in front of me." Miranda was already annoyed with her friend and she had been back mere hours.

Eve remained silent, glancing at Miranda's mom. Miranda cleared her throat.

"Let me save you the trouble, Eve," she said. "Mom, Eve, I think you'd both better sit for this one."

"Of course, dear. What is it?" Miranda's mom sat in the chair beside the bed as Eve sighed loudly, shaking her head.

Chapter Eighteen

By the time Miranda had finished her story of the underwater world, complete with Evan, Thomas, her father, Elise, and Abby, there was complete silence in the room.

She glanced anxiously back and forth from Eve to her mother, who were both sitting there, mouths hanging open.

"Well? Now do you see what's happened?" Miranda asked, twisting her hands.

Eve glanced at Miranda's mother, who nodded. Eve rose from her seat and backed out of the room.

"What? You don't believe me?" Miranda challenged, her voice rising.

"Honey, I hear these things are quite common. You've had quite the accident, perhaps even hit your head…" Her mother was rambling, avoiding eye contact.

"You *don't* believe me." Miranda attempted to get out of bed.

A nurse rushed in holding a paper cup and a pill.

"Miranda, dear. Calm down, you're distraught. Take this, it will relax you." The nurse came closer, handing her the water and medication.

"Get away from me. It happened! You guys have to believe me!"

"You need to calm down or I will call the doctor, who will insist that you take this pill," the nurse said firmly.

Taking a deep breath, Miranda willed herself to relax. The last thing she needed was to be drugged here at the hospital. She needed to go home, far from this beach. But what about her father? How could she help him?

"Mom, we need to help Dad. He's trapped, held prisoner by that awful mermaid."

"Honey, please. I'll try your father again. Will you calm down if I reach him?" Her mother asked.

"I...I guess." Miranda figured it would be a start. But she had other things on her mind as well. "I also need to speak with Evan, privately."

"Ethan. His name is Ethan." Eve walked back into the room, a frown on her face.

"I don't care what his name is, bring him in here now!" Miranda bellowed.

"I don't think he's ready to have this conversation. He's a little freaked out—not that I can blame him," Eve explained.

"Eve, bring him in here," Miranda's mom commanded. Eve spun on her heels and left the room once more.

"Thank you, Mom. He'll understand." Miranda wanted to touch him, speak with him.

"I don't know about that, dear. I wouldn't overwhelm him. I feel that you've had a bad dream, a nightmare perhaps..." Thinking back to all those nights without sleep, Miranda considered the possibility and then brushed the thought aside.

Miranda's mother was interrupted by the sound of Ethan walking in the room. He looked as pale as a ghost.

"Miranda, honey, I think you should just get some rest."

"Mom, please. I need to see him, privately, I'm begging you." Miranda's fists were clenched at her sides.

Clearing his throat, he stood there until the nurse pulled Miranda's mother by the elbow, leading them out of the room.

Ethan stood, feet planted to the floor. Miranda recognized the look of fear written all over his face and knew that somehow he didn't remember.

"Evan—I mean Ethan. Sit." She gestured for him to sit in the chair beside her bed. Cautiously he approached Miranda and took a seat.

"Ethan. Let's start over again, okay?" Miranda had to remain calm, otherwise she would scare him away. "Please listen to me with an open mind, okay?"

Nodding, Ethan swallowed hard.

"You and I knew each other, very well. In fact, we were in love." Miranda saw his face change from pale white to red in a matter of seconds. "Now hear me out. You were with me, in this beautiful underwater world with mermaids. You *were* one—a merman, that is."

Ethan sprang quickly to his feet. Miranda leaned over and pushed down on his arm. He sat once more, his eyes wide.

"I thought you were going to be a prisoner forever. I thought that I would never see you again. I can't believe that she let you go." Miranda gazed into those gray eyes and longed for him to remember something, anything.

"I...Miranda, I think you're really pretty and sweet and everything, but I don't have a clue what you're talking about." This time he stood and walked to the door. "I think you need to rest. I'll be back later, okay?"

Miranda bit her lip, knowing that it was a long shot that she would ever see him again. She sank back into her bed. Nobody believed her, nobody.

Miranda's mother walked back into the room, a cautious look in her eyes. "Miranda, it's your father. I got him on the line." Sitting up, Miranda snatched her mother's cell phone from her hand as she felt her heart race in her chest.

"Daddy! Speak to me!" Miranda exclaimed. It was her father, all right, and he sounded just fine. Speaking in hushed tones, Miranda asked him if he recalled anything about their ordeal.

"Honey, you need to get some rest. You've been through so much. I'll be there tomorrow and we'll talk, but no, I just needed to clear my head, get away for a few days. I'm fine."

Handing the phone back to her mother after disconnecting the call, Miranda was amazed that she was the only one who could remember.

"Mom? When did things start going bad between you and Dad?"

"I…I don't know. Now is really not the time for this."

"Please? When did you see things start to go bad?"

"Miranda, really? Now?" Miranda's mom was growing impatient, her voice rising.

"I was young, right? Maybe you were even pregnant with me?" Miranda urged.

The shock on her mother's face spoke volumes. She had hit the nail on the head.

"I *knew* it!" she shouted.

"Miranda, what does it matter? Why does any of this matter? Your father loved you, right from the start. Whatever has been going on with you guys these last few months has been killing him. Let it go. Sarah's not the enemy," her mother pleaded.

"Oh, I could care less about Sarah now—and you're right, she's *not* the enemy. Abby is." Miranda smacked her lips together.

"Okay, there you go again. I'm calling the doctor." Her mom paced the room, her hands flailing. "I don't know what to do anymore."

Knowing that continued talk of the mermaid would only be met with the threat of medication, Miranda decided to give it a rest—at least until her dad arrived. "Fine, Mom. You're probably right. It was most likely just a huge, horrible nightmare."

"Good! Now no more nonsense about mermaids and prisoners, okay?"

"Yup." Miranda feigned agreement.

"Whew. Now, I'm going to grab some coffee. Would you like something?'

"Nope, I'm good. I've got my snacks, everything is great." She plastered a smile on her face. Her mother squinted at her from across the room.

"Hmm. Are you sure?"

"Absolutely, Mom." *Now, to wait until Dad arrives.*

***

There were no more visits from Ethan. When Miranda questioned Eve about him and Theo, Eve changed the subject. How could she just pretend that the love of her life was nothing to her?

But she had to play the game, otherwise her mother would worry and she'd never get out of the hospital.

The next day, her father arrived in the late afternoon.

"Miranda! Thank goodness you're all right." Her dad rushed to wrap her in a hug.

"Dad, it's you! It's really you!" The sight of him brought fresh tears to her eyes. She had heard his voice on the phone, but she couldn't rest until she saw him with her very own eyes. "Where were you the last few days?"

"Oh. Funny thing: I kind of got cold feet, I guess. Weird thing is, I didn't see it coming." Her dad scratched his head, his gaze resting on the floor.

"I thought you loved Sarah, Dad."

"I do, I guess. Honey, this whole Sarah thing has caused so much tension between the two of us that I just needed some space." His brows scrunched.

"Dad, where have you been? Where did you stay the past few days?"

"I...I drove around."

This was getting stranger by the moment. "Drove around? For several days?" She frowned. "Is there anything else that you remember—anything at all?"

"I don't recall much else except wanting to get away. I've been thinking, Miranda. If you'd prefer, I won't marry Sarah."

"*What?* Of course you should marry her. I was being obnoxious." Sarah was an angel compared to that undersea witch.

"You sure? You seemed so..." Her dad floundered for the correct word.

"Wrong, bratty, jealous?" Miranda wished more than anything that she could go back in time and correct her behavior. "Admit it, Dad. I was awful and I'm sorry—to you and to Sarah. As a matter of fact, I was pretty awful to lots of people." In her head, Miranda rattled off some names: Sarah, her mother, Eve...

"Now hold on, Miranda. There's a fair share of blame to go around here. I could have been more tactful, understanding." Miranda's dad gazed at her, pushing her hair to the side.

"Oh, Dad. Are you really okay?" Miranda's eyes welled up with tears.

Her father leaned closer to hug her. "I am now. What do you say we start over, forget about the past few months?"

Breathing in his clean, fresh scent, Miranda wanted nothing more than to erase the past and start anew. Lingering thoughts of Evan and Elise filled her brain, the only people that she would be missing in her life. They were once so very important. Could it have been a dream? She supposed that it was possible; maybe her imagination had gotten the best of her. But then where had Dad been these last few days? He couldn't even answer that question himself.

If it were, indeed a dream, that would mean that her love with Evan had never happened. Maybe she remembered seeing him on the beach that night before she drowned and had conjured up an underwater romance filled with danger, intrigue, and mystery. Miranda's mother and teachers had always claimed that she had an outstanding imagination. There were so many unanswered questions, so many loose ends.

"When will you see Sarah again?" Miranda needed to apologize to her, too, and try her best to give Sarah a chance.

"I'm heading back tomorrow, as long as the doctors feel you're okay to leave."

"Thanks, Dad. Do you think it would be all right if I drove back with you?" Above all, Miranda wanted to spend time with her father. They had missed so much precious time together.

"As long as it's okay with your mother. What about Eve?"

"I'm sure she can handle a drive home with Mom. The two of them love each other." Miranda giggled.

"I'm going to head back to the hotel for a while and get some rest. I feel like these past few days have taken their toll on me. I'll be back in the morning to pick you up." Her father reached over to kiss the top of her head.

* * *

"Dr. Samuels, are you positive that Miranda is able to leave tomorrow morning? I mean, she's been saying strange things, acting different."

Miranda could hear the hushed whispers coming from outside of the hallway. Her mother was talking to the doctor again. She should have known better than to spill her guts and apologize to her mom for her negative attitude the past year or so. Her behavior must have been pretty bad in order for her mother to be this shocked by an apology.

Coming into the room, Miranda's mom was stone-faced while the doctor wore a grin.

"How are we feeling today, Miranda? Mom tells me you've been a bit emotional." Checking her pulse and listening to her heartbeat with his stethoscope, the older man grinned.

"I thought that it would be nice to apologize for the way I've been acting lately. I guess after what I've been through, I'm learning to appreciate the people and things in my life more." Miranda meant every word, but she also wanted out of this hospital. She had decided to let the underwater fantasy go. No more talk of mermaids, being held prisoner, or Evan.

"Makes perfect sense to me." The doctor winked at Miranda, then turned to face her mother. "You see, sometimes when people go through a traumatic event, they react in many different ways. I would say this reaction is quite a positive one."

"Yes, but what about the outlandish stories of an underwater world? Or that poor boy Ethan she claims to have had a relationship with when he was a merman, for goodness's sake!" Miranda's mother placed her head in her hands.

Miranda felt embarrassed. She had been a fool to voice her feelings when she first came out of it, and she was never going to live this down.

Just then, Eve, Ethan, and Theo entered. Her heart practically leapt out of her chest at the sight of Ethan. *Play it cool.*

The doctor touched her mother's elbow. "Miranda, you can expect to leave tomorrow morning. You look fine to me. Just get some rest tonight," he called as they walked out of the room.

"Wow. It'll be nice to go home and let everything get back to normal." Eve approached her, a smile playing on her lips, but the circles under her friend's eyes told a different story.

'Yeah, I guess it will be nice. It wasn't much of a birthday, was it?" Miranda's eyes met Eve's as the girls giggled softly.

"It was certainly eventful. Listen, Theo and I are going to grab something in the cafeteria. Do you want anything?"

Miranda's mom had just brought some fresh fruit and a sandwich. "Nah, I'm good." She waved as the two left.

It was just Miranda and Ethan now.

"I...I wanted to tell you that I'm sorry about scaring you," Miranda began. "It seems I've had some wild dream and you were one of the leading characters." She shrugged, feeling a faint blush rise to her face.

"It's fine, I understand. I should be flattered that I was part of your dream, I suppose."

The star, Miranda wanted to blurt out, but she knew better. The last thing she wanted to do was scare this boy off again. "Good, it's all good." The red heat was growing stronger as she gazed up at Ethan's striking eyes.

"Would you like to go out sometime, when you get home and get settled?" Ethan asked hesitantly.

"Home? Where do you live?" Her mother wouldn't be keen on the idea of driving her down to the shore for dates.

"I live a few towns over from you. Didn't Eve tell you?"

Why hadn't Eve told her this? "Oh, no, she didn't say anything." Miranda stammered. Wait a minute, Ethan was asking her out. *Ethan is asking me out!*

"Well?"

"I...yes." Miranda fumbled over her words. "I would like that."

"Good." Did she detect that Ethan was blushing as well? "Okay, then. My family and I are heading back tomorrow. Can I have your number?" He pulled out his cell phone and she recited it as he punched in the digits.

"I'll see you, then." Ethan wavered on his feet.

"Yes, I'm looking forward to it." Miranda said, a grin escaping from her lips.

"Bye, then." Ethan walked to the door.

"Ethan?" Miranda called out. He turned. "Thanks for saving my life."

"It was my pleasure." Ethan winked and headed out the door.

Chapter Nineteen

Three months later...

"I had a great time tonight." Ethan reached over, taking her hand. Miranda felt the warmth of his hand in hers, banishing the chill of the autumn evening,

"Me too." She would never grow tired of gazing into his gray eyes.

"I'm so glad I decided to save your life." Ethan's eyes lit up. It had been a private joke of theirs the last few months.

"I'm so glad you did, too." She leaned over to place a kiss on his soft mouth. She and Ethan had been dating since they had returned from the infamous vacation at the beach. Eve was also steadily dating Theo and the foursome had become quite tight. The boys live about fifteen minutes away, and they were able to arrange to meet most weekends.

"Do you ever think about what would have happened if you weren't there playing football with Theo that night?" Miranda had been thinking about this more and more lately. Would she have died? Would Eve and her mom have been able to save her, call for help in time?

"There's no point in thinking like that. We were meant to be together. You were meant to survive. It all worked out for a reason." Ethan ran his fingers through her long hair.

"Hm. You're right." Miranda knew she was destined to meet Ethan, whether in her dreams or in reality.

After several attempts to resurrect her memories of the mermaids, Miranda had finally called it quits. She had questioned her father several more times, asking if he thought her dream may have been rooted in reality. Her father had asked if she wanted to speak with a counselor. Eve had threatened to tell Miranda's mother if there was any more talk of mermaids. And Ethan—well, she didn't wish to scare him away like she had almost done back at the hospital.

Instead the memories were hers to cherish, and real or not, they had taught her a lesson: to appreciate what you have, to cherish your friends and family. Yes, there were days when she felt her attitude creeping up, but she was careful to treat those around her with kindness. Besides, how could the memories be real if her father was here on Earth with her? Knowing Abby, there was no way that she would have allowed Miranda's father to come back home—of that she was certain.

"Want to go to the movies next weekend?" Ethan asked.

"Sure. We can see if Eve and Theo want to join us, too."

Blinding lights shone in the driveway as Ethan's mom pulled her car in. The couple walked outside, and Miranda waited for Ethan's mom to roll the window down. "Hi, Mrs. Stevens."

"Hi, Miranda. Hope you two had fun. It's a beautiful evening."

"Want to come in for a while?" Miranda offered. Ethan's mom had become friendly with

Miranda's mom, and sometimes she came in for coffee.

"Maybe next time. Mr. Stevens is waiting for me back home. Tell her I said hi though."

"Will do. Bye, Mrs. Stevens. Bye, Ethan." Waving as the car pulled out of her driveway, Miranda stood for a moment and enjoyed the cool brisk air biting at her cheek.

The overhead light snapped Miranda out of her thoughts as she made her way to the front door.

"What are you doing just standing there? It's cold outside, come on in. I've got dinner ready."

* * *

"How are your classes coming along?" Miranda's mother asked for the millionth time since school had started. High school was so different from middle school. Here, Miranda felt more independence and a sense of achievement. With college only several years away, there was finally a purpose to all of this hard work.

"Good, Mom." Miranda groaned inwardly as she peered at the TV. Mom always chose moments right smack in the middle of a really awesome show to have a heart-to-heart.

"Are you and Eve still good? I know when I was in high school, some of my friends went different ways. It just happens."

"Mom. Eve is over almost every single day." She enunciated the words carefully, then recalled her new change of attitude. "Sorry, Mom. I'm just trying to watch this show, I've been waiting for it."

"Why don't you record it? I have a few minutes before I need to go shopping and I'd like to spend it talking to you."

Since when did Mom know about recording shows? Snatching the remote, Miranda pushed a few buttons and then powered the TV off. She forced a smile on her face. "Yes, Mom, Eve and I are great. School is great."

"Well, good. And Ethan? He seems like a very nice boy."

"Yes, Mom. He is." Somehow Miranda had a feeling that the real reason for this conversation had yet to come up. Tapping her fingers on her lap, she waited for her mom to continue.

"So your father's wedding is coming up soon." *I knew it.* "Are you okay with being in the wedding?"

Mom had picked a fine time to ask, with the wedding only weeks away. But she and Sarah had reached an understanding and had started their relationship on a clean slate.

"Yes, I'm good." Miranda didn't feel it necessary to go into detail about coming to terms with Sarah and the wedding.

Her mother glanced down at the floor, her mouth in a thin line.

"Mom, are *you* okay with it?"

"Me? Yeah, of course." But something in the way her mother's voice shook made Miranda think otherwise. It must be difficult to see your ex-husband get on with his life when you weren't even dating. Although Miranda had been trying to push any thoughts of Abby away, there had been that one conversation about how her father could never give his heart away again. Perhaps there was some truth to the imagined conversation.

"Mom. I don't think that Dad can love again. I mean *really* love again."

Her mother looked up, eyes wide. "Miranda, why on earth would you ever say such as thing?"

"I just have a feeling that after you guys lost your love for one another, he was never the same again."

"He was the one who left, Miranda. What are you saying?"

It wouldn't do any good to explain to her mom that a fictitious mermaid had convinced her that her father could never open his heart again, so Miranda tried to paraphrase.

"You guys were really happy once, weren't you? Think back to when you first met, when you first married."

Miranda's mom had a faraway look in her eyes, focusing on the past, on happy memories.

"I'm right, aren't I?" Watching her mom nod, Miranda continued. "He loved you, heart and soul. A love like that truly comes along once in a lifetime. Regardless of why Dad left, he can't quite recapture that feeling he had with you."

"Huh." Miranda's mother turned to face her. "How did you become so wise?"

What would her mother say if Miranda told her that a mermaid had taught her a lesson on true love?

"Maybe I'm just observant," she said at last. "I think it's time you get out there again and find that person that will make you feel alive, special." Miranda knew that her mother had plenty to offer someone and deserved to fall in love again.

"It sounds like you're speaking from experience, Miranda." Her mother's face revealed a small smile.

"Maybe I am." Ethan crept into her thoughts, as he often did.

"My little girl is growing up." Her mom reached out to touch her hair.

Feeling slightly embarrassed, Miranda rolled her eyes but a grin escaped.

Clearing her throat, Miranda's mom walked toward the front door. "Is there anything that you want from the store?" she asked, scooping up her keys.

"No thanks, Mom. I'm good." And she *was* good—better than she had been in a long time.

Chapter Twenty

One of the best results of Miranda's accident was becoming closer to her father. He and Sarah appeared to be okay with each other once again—yet another reason to discard the notion of Abby. As a shiver passed through Miranda's spine, she considered the fact that a world without Abby was a better one.

Abby had fooled her at first, drawing Miranda into her little web by acting silly, kind, and even caring at times. She was an intricate creature—how could Miranda have possibly imagined such a being and conjured her into her dreams? But if there was even the slightest possibility that her vivid dream had been real, how could her father and Ethan have escaped? Was it possible that her father's love actually softened Abby's heart? Broke through the ice?

Shaking her head, she brought herself back to reality. She was better off not wondering. It just made more sense to believe that the whole thing was a dream.

"Are you going with Sarah to her last fitting?" Miranda's dad popped his head into her bedroom.

Miranda had gone to the bridal store countless times with Sarah. Nothing against her, but it was getting boring, just standing around watching Sarah get fitted. On the other hand, Miranda didn't want Sarah to be by herself for this important part of the wedding process.

"Is she going alone?"

"Nah, she's got her mom and sister going with her."

"What are you going to do?"

"I'll figure something out. I might take in that movie." Her father loved action movies. So did Miranda.

"Would you like company?" she asked, placing her magazine down on her nightstand.

"Sure, that sounds like fun." Her father checked this watch. "We've got about an hour before we need to leave. Do you want to ask Eve if she'd like to join us?"

Moments alone with her dad were few and far between. "Nah, let's just go alone."

"Great! Don't forget. One hour."

"Got it."

* * *

Propping her pillow up, Miranda grabbed the remote. The movie with her dad had been great.

She flipped through the channels until the sound of her phone jarred her. Ethan.

Miranda's spirits lifted as they always did whenever he called. She snatched up her phone. "Hey. What's up?'

"I was just sitting here, thinking about you."

"Well, that makes both of us. What did you do tonight?" Miranda asked, flipping her blonde hair through her fingers.

"I just hung out here at the house. Theo and some of the other guys went to the mall, but I had a lot of work to do." One of the many things that she liked about Ethan was the fact that he was a conscientious student. He was wiser than his years, just as Evan had been. *There I go again.*

"I went to the movies with my dad," she said aloud. "Sarah had a fitting for her dress, so it was kind of cool having some time with my dad."

"So you're good with everything? Being in the wedding?"

"Yeah, Sarah's very cool. I feel bad that I put her through the wringer when I first met her. You're still coming too, right?"

"I wouldn't miss seeing you all dressed up in that green bridesmaid dress!" he teased.

"It's *not* green, it's teal. And it's not so bad," Miranda retorted.

"Yes, well, either way, I wouldn't miss it. I bet you're going to be the most beautiful girl there." His voice was soft, all traces of teasing gone.

Miranda felt butterflies in her stomach. *How does he have the ability to make me feel so special? Is it love?*

"Miranda? Did you hear what I said?'

Realizing that she had been daydreaming, Miranda cleared her throat. "Oh, sorry. What was it that you said?"

"I asked if you felt like we were destined to meet."

Placing a hand on her chest, her heart pounded wildly. "Evan..."

"It's Ethan, Miranda. Ethan."

What was wrong with her? Why did she call him Evan again? "I...I'm sorry. I...yes, I do believe..." Miranda stammered, feeling uneasy.

"Are you okay? You sound funny. I didn't mean to scare you."

"No, you didn't scare me, Ethan. It's just that you caught me off-guard, I guess. I feel the same way. I just never imagined..." The

[152]

conversation echoed so many she had shared with Evan, it was frightening her.

"Good. I mean, I feel like whatever happens from here, whatever our futures may bring, I doubt that I'll ever be able to feel the same way."

Sucking in a deep breath, Miranda felt light-headed. "I...I have to go, I'll call you later." Ending the call, she rocked herself in her bed. *It can't be, it can't be...*

The sound of a text coming through made her jump. It was Ethan.

"What did I do? Call me back."

Hugging herself, Miranda stared at her phone, willing him to just give her a moment to gather her thoughts. She had been making progress with her dream; she had been sure that it had never happened. But now why was Ethan talking like Evan? Was this how most teenage boys acted?

Grabbing her phone, she punched in a quick text to Eve.

"Get over here. Now."

"?" Eve responded.

"Please." Miranda knew that it was late, but she'd sneak down and open the door for Eve. Hopefully her mother wouldn't be the wiser.

She powered down her phone until she could figure out how to handle the conversation with Ethan. Tiptoeing past her mom's bedroom, she saw the lights from the TV stream out from under the door.

Before Eve had a chance to knock on the door—or worse, ring the doorbell—Miranda was downstairs waiting. Eve appeared within minutes.

"What is the matter with you. Have you gone insane? It's a school night."

Miranda closed the door behind her friend. "Shh!" she hissed through clenched teeth. "My mom will hear you."

She led her friend to the couch in the basement. "Do you and Theo ever talk about...love?" she managed.

"Love? Do we talk about *love*?" Eve's eyes were wide.

"Yes, answer the question." Miranda was growing impatient.

"Um, no, not yet. I mean, we're only fourteen!" Eve threw her hands up in the air.

"Just as I thought." Miranda wrung her hands, rising from the couch to pace the room. "Do you talk about destiny, fate?"

"Heck, no!" Eve's jaw dropped. "Is Ethan saying this stuff to you?" Now she was on her feet.

"Yes, he is! It just proves..." Miranda stopped.

"It just proves *what?*" Eve yelled.

Miranda was by her side in an instant, clamping her hand over her mouth. "Be quiet! Mom will hear you!"

"What is going on here?" Eve demanded.

"I...I think it's quite possible that Ethan is Evan." There, she said it. *Let Eve think I'm crazy. I'm tired of holding back my thoughts, my feelings.*

"*What!* Have you gone crazy? Where is your mother? I need to find her." Breaking away from Miranda, Eve headed for the stairs.

"Eve, don't! Please!" Miranda begged her friend.

Eve hesitated, then retreated to face Miranda. "Listen, I thought you were past this."

"I thought I was, too, but what other explanation could there be?" Miranda was at her wits' end. If Ethan was Evan, that meant that Abby was real, and Elise…

"Maybe he's just a weirdo. Have you ever thought of that?" Eve blurted. She grabbed Miranda's shoulders, shaking her.

A weirdo? Miranda supposed it was possible. She relaxed for the first time since she had spoken with Ethan. "A weirdo. Yes, he's just a weirdo." Giggling now, she grabbed her friend.

"Okay, you're freaking me out." Eve backed two steps away.

"No, it's fine. I'm good. I was just overreacting, that's all."

"Okay, so can I leave now?' Eve asked in a whisper.

"Yes, go ahead. I'll talk to you tomorrow." Miranda walked a silent Eve to the door. Watching her friend cross the driveway, she waved. *All was right with the world.*

Miranda headed back up to the bedroom. It was safe to power up her phone again. Miranda had received two more messages from Ethan asking her to call him, a sense of urgency to his words. Shaking her head, she laughed as she found Ethan's name and prepared to call him back.

He's just a sensitive teenage boy in love. That she could handle. Determined to let it go, Miranda was now back in a safe place, tucked in her bed, far from the clutches of Abby, the dream-induced mermaid.

Epilogue

"Are you ready?" Sarah brushed a stray piece of hair out of her eyes. "You look beautiful."

"You, too. Sarah. I mean it." Miranda adjusted her teal taffeta dress, pulling at the sash. Scrunching her face in the mirror, she figured the dress wasn't *that* bad. She had seen a lot worse.

Sarah, on the other hand, shone in a straight, off-the-shoulder ivory gown. The ivory contrasted with her long dark hair, making her skin glow. Gazing at Sarah's reflection behind her in the mirror, Miranda squeezed her hand on her shoulder.

"What do you say in a situation like this again? Break a leg?" Miranda chuckled, turning to face Sarah.

"Something like that. Thank you, Miranda, for everything." Leaning in to embrace her, Sarah wiped a tear from her eye. Miranda nodded and urged her to head to the church.

Miranda and Sarah had become close the past few months. Remembering when she had resented her place in her life, Miranda was glad that she had let Sarah into her heart. Sarah had turned out to be kind and understanding, almost like a big sister.

Miranda met up with the rest of the wedding party, eager for the ceremony to begin. The man playing the piano was warming up, fiddling with the keys. Breathing deeply, Miranda spied Ethan, Eve, and Theo in the pews. Blowing a kiss back at Ethan, Miranda straightened her posture. Yes, Ethan was a eager teen boy in love, that was all.

Pulling at her sash, she fidgeted, feeling her bare neckline. She probably should have taken the time to pick out a necklace that complemented her dress. Finally, the piano came to life with a loud rendition of the wedding march.

Gazing straight ahead, Miranda took her cue and headed down the aisle, arm in arm with her groomsman, a friend of her father's from many years ago. Sweat poured off her face, and she wondered why the church suddenly felt so warm. She felt herself relax as she found her place near the altar. As she watched the next couple make their way to the front, Miranda felt genuine happiness for her dad and Sarah.

The ceremony was short and sweet, her father and Sarah reciting their vows and professing their love for each other. Miranda paid close attention to the words her father spoke, pleased to hear that they sounded sincere. *Take that, Abby,* Miranda smirked. All was right with the world again. The married couple sealed the deal with a lingering kiss met with applause.

Afterward, Miranda met her wedding partner and returned down the aisle, smiling as she met Ethan's eyes. In the back room, she collected her things. She imagined holding Ethan close, dancing to the slow songs at the reception tonight. Other members of the wedding party filtered into the room, and the soft buzz of chatter filled the air.

Ethan, Eve, and Theo appeared.

"You looked great!" Eve grabbed her in a hug. Ethan approached her other side.

Eve fumbled with her purse, and pulled out a small white box. "Your mom forgot to give you this. I ran into her after she dropped you off in the parking lot."

Confusion knit Miranda's brows as she slowly opened the box. A shimmering turquoise jewel sparkled on a chain.

"What is it, Miranda?" Eve asked.

"What...where..." Miranda stammered, desperate to clear her thoughts. "Where did my mom get this from?" she finally managed.

"Beats me. She said she thought it would look pretty with your dress, I have to agree with her." Eve reached out to touch the jewel.

Ethan picked it up, twirling the chain through his hands, his eyes wide. "You were wearing this that night on the beach, when I saved you."

Miranda's mind scrambled. How did her mother get this necklace? Maybe she had removed it at the hospital and forgotten about it until now.

"I kind of remember that, now that you mention it." Eve's voice sounded as if it were coming from a tunnel, faraway and muffled.

Miranda's mind was reaching for the memory. What was it that Evan had said that very first time they had kissed under the sea? He had known that the gift was from Abby and Elise.

Of course, now she remembered.

"Ethan..." Miranda felt herself waver. His eyes were still focused on the necklace. She needed to breathe. "Ethan..."

"This type of beauty only comes from the sea," Ethan whispered, eyes fixed on the jewel.

Miranda pulled Ethan's sleeve, her heart racing. Slowly, he gazed down at her. Their eyes locked.

About the author

Mya O'Malley was born and raised in the suburbs of New York City, where she currently lives with her husband, daughter and three stepdaughters. The family also consists of two boxers; Destiny and Dolce and a ragdoll cat named Colby. Mya earned an undergraduate degree in special education and a graduate degree in reading and literacy. She works as a special education teacher and enjoys making a difference in the lives of her students.

Mya's passion is writing; she has been creating stories and poetry since she was a child. Mya spends her free time reading just about anything she can get her hands on. She is a romantic at heart and loves to create stories with unforgettable characters. Mya likes to travel; she has visited several Caribbean Islands, Mexico and Costa Rica. Other releases include *At First Sight, Where There is Love, and If You Believe*. Mya is currently working on her sixth novel.

Other Solstice titles you might enjoy…

Always & Forever
By: Diana Harrison

Jon Burton thinks he's having a nightmare but the bad dreams don't fade when he's awake.

Callie, his girlfriend, mother of his son Oliver, has been killed in a road accident.

Now he faces life as a single parent.

He's at school taking his A levels.

He wants to go to Uni.

His mother has her own life and career.

His sister, Fay, older and wiser perhaps' advises him to have the baby adopted. Get on with his life.

He should do that.

Callie doesn't want him to do that. Only her body is dead. Her spirit is still alive. And she wants Jon, Oliver, and her to stay together.

Always & Forever.

Breathless
By: S.D. Grimm

Eighteen year old Claire Summers has a rare gift she must keep secret, she's a Breather. When she touches an object someone else has touched, she sees that person's memories. When she stumbles across a memory of her friend in danger, she'll do anything to help rescue him. The problem is, her secret will be revealed. If the wrong people find out about her ability, they'll hunt her, because Breathers are powerful weapons.

Healer
By: J. McAfee

A routine trip to the hardware store plunges Grace into a whirlwind of supernatural forces and impossible choices. Life as she knows it is changed in an instant when she encounters a Master Demon who confronts her with her tragic past. Battling for her sanity is the first step in a series of tumultuous events as she rediscovers her link to a dwindling ancient race. Sworn to protect humanity from the forces of evil, the last remaining Knowers must break a centuries-old edict and join forces with a rag tag group of mortals to defend against a dark army sweeping the planet. Along the way, Grace discovers the unseen arts and is challenged to stretch her secret abilities further than ever before.

For more Solstice titles, visit our online store:
www.solsticepublishing.com/bookstore

Made in the USA
Middletown, DE
13 January 2015